Gerald Nathanson was born in London. Due to WW2 he was evacuated three times and went to eleven schools. At age eighteen he volunteered for National Service in the RAF and became a medic in Bomber Command.

He married at the age of 26, and had two sons. He became a London taxi driver, and Blue Badge tourist guide. His wife and both his sons supported him when he joined Birkbeck College at the age of 74 and graduated with a BA Hons, Student of the year Award, at the age of 78. Since retirement he has taken up writing.

To John & ...

To THE LADIES IN THE DELI

From

Gerald

I dedicate this book to my wife Carole, and my sons, Adam and Gavin.

Gerald Nathanson

The Chess Board Execution and other stories

AUSTIN MACAULEY PUBLISHERS™

LONDON • CAMBRIDGE • NEW YORK • SHARJAH

A CIP catalogue record for this title is available from the British Library.

ISBN 9781398441750 (Paperback)
ISBN 9781398441767 (ePub e-book)

www.austinmacauley.com

First Published 2022
Austin Macauley Publishers Ltd®
1 Canada Square
Canary Wharf
London
E14 5AA

I would like to acknowledge the influence of Professor Sue Jackson, who first introduced me to Birkbeck College, where I fulfilled an impossible dream.

TIS

'Tis all a chequerboard of nights and days where destiny with men for pieces plays;

"Hither and Thither moves, and mates, and slays. And one by one back in the Closet lays".

From "Old Song" by Edward Fitzgerald.

Prologue
1943

For two hours they stood dressed in their thin striped prison clothes, a thousand shivering prisoners had waited since 6 am, on this cold Wednesday morning in January 1943 not daring to move, they stood in line for the roll call, a routine daily check to see if any of the prisoners had managed to escape or had died during the night. This roll call took place every morning before they could run to the food tables which were open for one hour only. The whistle sounded, a shrill sound, echoing across the grounds of this concentration camp, it seemed to waken these statuesque figures into life. A signal for the prisoners, men, women and children, to run across a large compound, they pushed shoved and shouted, their voices, were a cacophony of languages from all over Europe, from the east to the west. French, Dutch, German, Polish, Russian. They ran across part of the compound known as the gauntlet of death. The commandant of the Schlossberg Concentration Camp sat in his comfortable chair, his young twin daughters and his son sat beside him as he randomly took shots with his gun at the prisoners running this gauntlet, dragging along their children by their tiny cold blue hands, and trying to protect them. The commandant and his children were warmly wrapped up against this bitter cold winter's morning, and they laughed as the victims of this sadistic, random killing game fell, either dead or wounded. 'Over there, Papa,' said his son Dedrik, pointing to a tight group of prisoners trying to escape the bullets. His daughters' Gudrun and Erma, likewise selected victims for their father's gun. The sound of the gun being fired was lost over the screams of the prisoners.

Among the victims this day running to those food tables were a family of five, of which only the eight-year-old son managed to escape into the crowd, taking a scared and horrified look at his family's murderer and the murderer's children.

'Mama, Papa,' the little boy screamed, as his parents and sisters fell to the ground. The boy, Gershon, was pulled away, by friendly hands grabbing his arms as he tried to free himself in the struggle and go to his dead family.

Chapter One
1970

It was on Monday eighth June 1970 when there was a shout, 'Inspector, inspector,' the cries from a policeman, as he ran along the corridor in the Rue Philippe Police Station in Antwerp. 'Inspector,' he called again, but louder. Faces emerged from doorways in the corridor, alarmed by the urgency in the voice. A door at the far end of the corridor was flung open and Inspector Arnaude Babineaux appeared, puzzled by the shouting, only to be confronted by one of his police officers, who, with a strained white-face and very agitated, practically fell into the arms of the inspector. 'Raphael,' said the inspector, as he approached this police officer. 'Keep calm.' Babineaux placed his hands on the distressed policeman's shoulder to steady him and guided him into his office. Once inside, he asked Raphael what the panic was about, but the inspector, sitting on the edge of his desk had to wait as Constable Raphael fell into a large deep brown, leather padded armchair, one of two set aside for private meetings with senior officers. Policemen did not usually sit down in his office, without an invitation, however, because of the frenetic state of this policeman, Raphael, Inspector Babineaux said nothing until he managed to calm him. But he too became disturbed and deeply upset when the policeman related to him the reason for his mad dash through the police station on the Rue Philippe.

Raphael reported to the inspector of a shooting that had taken place in the prestigious Royal Leopold Luxury Apartments, situated on the Avenue Rue de Liberation in the suburb district of Antwerp. Raphael knew, as did many of the officers in this police station, that the inspector played chess every week with the owner of the apartment where the shooting had taken place.

Inspector Babineaux, accompanied by armed policemen, was driven at breakneck speed to the Royal Leopold Apartments. With his men trying to keep up with him, Babineaux ran through a crowd of inquisitive onlookers who had gathered in the street as soon as word had spread of a shooting in these three apartments. He burst into the building, cursing the wait while the lift descended from the upper floors.

Arriving at the eighth floor, where the shooting had taken place, Babineaux and his men were met by a uniformed policeman guarding the entrance to one of three very luxurious apartments, the door of which was hanging precariously by its three broken hinges. The policeman on guard outside the apartment, on seeing and recognising the inspector, lowered his hold on the gun in his hand, and explained that he and his colleagues had had to break down the door to gain access to the apartment. He then nodded and pointed to the large dining room behind him where there were several policemen who had been examining the apartment had expressed themselves puzzled by its tidiness. Nothing was disturbed or damaged, just three people sitting at the dining table; a woman and two children, both blonde girls, apparently twins, about three years of age, all shot in the back of the head. In an adjoining room of similar size, a dead man sat on a well upholstered office chair, at a desk in what seemed to be a very elaborate and expensively decorated library, the existence of which was previously unknown to the inspector. The dead man, the owner of the apartment, was the inspector's friend, Gershon Marcovitch.

The inspector went into all the other rooms and confirmed, what the policemen searching apartment had said, that nothing had been disturbed. The inspector was puzzled by the fact that whenever he and Gershon Marcovitch played chess together, in this apartment, it was always played in the lounge, as if this more appropriate part of the flat did not exist. Had Gershon deliberately kept this room a secret from his friend? That was the impression made upon Inspector Babineaux, and he asked himself what secrets this room held and why was he now feeling so apprehensive about what might be discovered.

In the centre of the library room stood a round, beautifully made antique coffee table, upon which lay a well-worn attaché case. Atop the attaché case sat a primitive looking wooden chess board which appeared to have been made from strips of scrap wood. Small holes had been cut into the squares to hold the chess pieces which had tiny pegs attached to fit the holes. This was not the handsome board on which the inspector and his friend had played chess. Inspector Babineaux was puzzled by the way in which the ten chess pieces were positioned on the board, was this a statement, giving the smallest value piece, the pawn, the most power to checkmate a black king. Supported by his white king, the white pawn could checkmate the black king, while the Bishop was in position for the coup-de-grace 4.

The positions on the chess board were black king b8, black pawn a7, white pawn c7, white king d7, black pawn g7, black pawn h7, white pawn a3, white Bishop f3, white pawn b2.

Babineaux was a keen chess player; he had regularly played with Gershon Marcovitch, and for over twelve years they had been friends and competitors in chess. They had first met when Gershon, a well-known diamond trader, had asked Inspector Babineaux for advice in securing his stocks of diamonds and other precious jewels, as well as documents.

Again, Babineaux studied the chess pieces on the board and only then noticed the swastika on some of them. He knew that Gershon was sending him a message, but what was it? He opened the attaché case, and extracted a large envelope addressed to himself which he opened immediately. Inside the envelope were several letters in Gershon's handwriting and what amounted to a retrospective account by a man who was determined not to forget the traumatic past which was to torment him throughout his life.

Skimming through the pages quickly, Babineaux read of war crimes which had gone unpunished and for which Gershon wanted justice to be done. But he was shocked and disturbed to read that in addition to the deaths in the apartment, two further deaths had taken place which awaited discovery. And then he read another handwritten page, which appeared more recent than the others, and which revealed instructions on how to unlock a safe hidden behind his collection of books. The instructions included the code to unlock the combination to the safe; 1, 9, 4 and 3 (1943). But first, the safe had to be found. The bodies of Gershon Marcovitch, his wife and the two children were taken away to the mortuary. There were tears on the inspector's face as the bodies were removed.

Babineaux estimated that there were probably about three thousand books spread over the bookcase lined walls. The books were arranged meticulously in order of subject; astronomy, business, ethics, gemmology, literature from around the world, religion, science, and more, all as might have been expected. A whole shelf in one bookcase was entirely dedicated to the German attitude to, and treatment of, Jews before, during and after World War Two, and the countries which had supported anti-Semitism then and since. Many of the books in the bookcases were beautifully bound and clearly valuable, as were the bookcases themselves.

Gershon would have known that the first senior officer to attend a terror related incident or a homicide in that district would be Babineaux. He was entrusting the search for the safe to his dear friend. The inspector was quite sure that it was not money or jewels that Gershon was protecting, because Gershon would have known how to deal with those. He was determined to find the safe and try to answer or carry out the requests Gershon asked of him, and he would do it by himself.

Over the course of many hours Babineaux removed each book from the shelves, as he did so, he marvelled at the beauty of the books and at his friend's erudition. He recognised very few of the books until he came to the literature section. When he took down the book "Foucault's Pendulum", he saw behind it a small pendulous handle, in the shape of a child's hand. He pulled it gently. His heart thumped as a section of the bookcase started to move towards him. He quickly cleared the books on either side as he continued to tug at the little hand; the back of the bookcase slid away. He saw a glimpse of metal, but he had to clear more shelves until he could remove the section of the bookcase to reveal a safe set in the wall behind it. Despite his wish to examine the safe further, Babineaux took the precaution of having witnesses to his next moves.

He therefore refrained from opening the safe until he was accompanied by two of his officers. But then a third man burst into the room and told Babineaux that that there had been two more killings, a man and a woman who had also been shot in the back of their heads. He shocked the police officer by saying, 'Yes, I had been expecting that.' He opened the safe and out fell a German officer's uniform with the name of the owner sewn into the lining of the jacket, SS Werner Hass, commandant of the Schlossberg Concentration Camp. Babineaux and his officers stood transfixed as they looked at this apparition of the past, and of the horrific memory of those millions of innocent people murdered, recalled, and represented by this German uniform now lying before them on the library floor. This German uniform encapsulated metaphorically that ghostly past. Babineaux arranged for the room to be sealed and set two of his men to guard the apartment with orders not to allow anyone to enter without his permission. Over the next few days every item in the safe was listed and papers copied many times, the originals carefully stored.

He decided to convene a meeting in this apartment attended by his superior officers, members of the judiciary as well as military officials who had attended the Nuremburg Trials between November 1945 and October 1946.

It took Inspector Arnaude Babineaux two weeks to convene the meeting which was held in Gershon's library on Monday 22nd June. Amongst this assembly of men there was one woman, Babineaux secretary, who was herself a policewoman. He told them to make themselves comfortable because he expected that they might be in this apartment all day, maybe all night. He seated the men in a semi-circle and facing the chair in which Gershon had died.

Babineaux then stood and looked at this legal assembly, waiting for them to settle down and then said, 'I will produce letters, show you documents and photographs and other items relating to five deaths or, as I first described them, executions. Because of the complexity and importance of this case, I have engaged my secretary to record everything that is said, which I hope, gentlemen, you will agree with.' He went on to address them further. 'I, Inspector Arnaude Babineaux, as a senior police officer of this district, have arrived at the most difficult situation in my whole career. I have no power to pass judgment, or to condemn, which is why, here, and now, I look to you for guidance, but also for justice. In the safe which is in this room, and which I opened two weeks ago, I found what amounts to a man's confession to the murder of five people and then his own suicide. The dead cannot stand trial, but the facts must be established, did Gershon Marcovitch commit murder, or did he carry out a justified execution? I will therefore take the opportunity you have kindly given me to present the case of the late Gershon Marcovitch. I ask you please to read the letters and the written record in front of you which were, I have every reason to believe, entrusted to me in the cause of justice. You will have to weigh up the pain of a traumatised eight-year-old child who saw his family slaughtered in front his eyes and who, by the strangest twist of fate, found himself, in later life, deeply involved with his family's torturers and murderers.'

Chapter Two
Gershon's Letter to Babineaux

"Before you start to read the letters and the other documents, I will introduce you to the names of Gershon's parents and his sisters."

'Gershon's father was called Chaim and his mother was Esther. He had two sisters, Zelda and Freda. Chaim was a competitive chess player and seven taught his family the intricacies of the chess board which resulted in the children being quite competent and competitive chess players from an early age.'

The assembled group of men listened as Babineaux began to read Gershon's diary and letters. 'Between the years 1940–1942, 76,000 Jews in France were deported, mostly from Paris. By the end of the war only 2,500 French Jews survived. I was one of many orphans among the survivors. My family came from Paris, and we were taken to the internment camp at Drancy; there were other internment camps in France at Compiegne, Pithiviers and Beaune-La-Rolande. In 1941, my family and I were transported from Drancy to the Schlossberg Concentration Camp in Germany. The Camp commandant was SS Sturmbannführer, (Lieutenant Colonel) Werner Hass.'

'My father had been in the furniture trade before the war and was a successful cabinet maker. He belonged to the Guild of Carpenters and Cabinet Makers and was highly regarded in the community. But one night our front door was kicked open and we were forced into the street. All the Jews were being rounded up and removed from their homes with little more than the clothes that they were wearing. We were piled into trucks and then into densely crowded trains in which we travelled, cold and hungry for what seemed to me like days. On arrival in the camp, we were made to line up to be "classified", all jewellery and any clothes of value removed and then we were tattooed with numbers on our arms and given striped "prison" clothing. We were in a concentration camp.

When allowed out during the day my father picked up pieces of discarded wood and bits of fallen trees. At night, in his bunk bed, he worked on the wood with a knife that he had secreted when we were arrested, and he made a small chess board. To make black chess pieces he stained the wood with urine and etched a small swastika on them, to represent the SS Guards, the white pieces represented my family and other prisoners in the camp.'

'The inmates in this prison hut, many of whom could play chess, made wonderful use of the chess board that my father had made, and they helped him to hide it from the SS guards. Had that chess board been found, or any other form of pleasure to pass away the time come to light, it would certainly have resulted in a severe beating, or even death.'

Nobody asked any questions; the silence was palpable, broken only by the rustling of papers being passed from one to the other and the striking of matches, lighting up cigarettes

20

in the increasingly smoky room. Babineaux, had stopped reading, instead he watched as they continued to read the letters and documents which he had duplicated and in which Gershon described the daily life, if life is what it could be called, in the Schlossberg Concentration Camp. Even as a young child, Gershon was gifted with a photographic and indelible memory, so that even though he could not write about it at the time, he was able later to recall events with great precision. He wrote of the daily ritual of Commandant Werner Hass, always Luger gun in hand, who would often be seen sitting outside his office with his twin daughters, Gudrun and Erma, and his son Dedrik. Gershon clearly recalled that all the Hass children had blonde hair, very bright blonde hair.

It was on Monday the 17th of July 1944, when the prisoners turned out as usual at six o'clock in the morning but there were no SS guards and no commandant. In the distance they could hear gunfire, and while they were still trying to make sense of the situation, the prison gates were forced open and in marched Russian soldiers, smiling and singing. But the singing soon stopped, and the smiles quickly disappeared at the sight that confronted them. Walking skeletons, too ill, too tired, too confused to realise that these men in uniform were their liberators.

Rivers of tears flowed across the compound of death; soldiers helped to serve the weakest with food, whilst Russian army medics did what they could to treat the frail and wounded inmates and remove the bodies of those who had died during the night in their bunks. Later they would bury them but could give little more dignity than their oppressors had done. Teams of doctors and nurses arrived two days later to treat cases of malnutrition, tuberculosis, skin infections and the multitude of illnesses and diseases which starvation and ill-treatment had caused them to suffer. As soon as possible clean clothes were provided to replace the lice-ridden prison garments of the survivors. Some clothes were taken from the barracks of the fleeing German soldiers. The few Germans who were hiding were rounded up and received no mercy from the Russians.

The communities in the surrounding German villages to the Schlossberg concentration camp denied knowledge of the death camp when they were questioned about its existence and suffered the humiliation of having their homes ransacked for food and clothing by the Russian soldiers, which were then distributed among the survivors in the concentration camp. Those same German people were ordered to dig graves and bury the bodies of those men, women and children that had died through diseases, and malnutrition, or had been killed by the SS guards.

Accommodation had to be found for these liberated survivors, as the huts that they had been living in was infested with all types of contagious diseases, body waste and dirt. The German bunkers, barracks and shelters were a temporary measure of accommodation, until more suitable facilities could be arranged. Many Jews who had survived the death camps did not want to return to their homelands such as Poland, Austria, France, and Germany where they had been treated so brutally and where, they knew, there would be no homes waiting for them. Orphaned children, like Gershon, with no immediate traceable family were sent to countries that could accommodate them. many went to Switzerland, to temporary accommodation. Some lucky ones were reunited with family or friends with the assistance from the Jewish

Agency and other charities set up for that purpose. Others were dispersed around the world wherever there was a family or an institution to take them in. It was learnt from Gershon's own written record, that he was eventually transferred to a Jewish orphanage in Belgium, where he was well cared for and educated. After leaving school, Gershon was offered an apprenticeship with a prominent jeweller in Antwerp, Mordechai Steinberg.

Mordechai Steinberg, and his wife, their daughter Adele and son Benjamin treated Gershon as part of the family and insisted that he move out of the orphanage and come to live with them. Gershon grew into a quiet, serious man and Mordechai taught him everything there was to know about lapidary, fine jewellery design and stone setting, especially how to cut diamonds and bring out the brilliance of this precious gem, also how this hard mineral was used in industry, particularly in drilling. Mordechai guided Gershon through the intricacies of the business side of the jewellery trade. Gershon often accompanied Mordechai when he attended trade events around the world. As Gershon grew older and more experienced and confident in the jewellery trade and dealership he often represented the family business around the world on his own. To Mordechai and his wife, he was another son. On Gershon's twenty-seventh birthday the Steinberg family gave him a present; it was a partnership in the family business. The company then became Steinberg and Marcovitch. Gershon was rich and successful, but he often seemed withdrawn and lonely, Mordechai, loved him dearly, and understood that Gershon still mourned the loss of his family.

All this came to be revealed to the learned men attending the meeting in Gershon's apartment. They asked no questions, but every so often Babineaux would draw their attention to a document or read a letter out loud or show them photos. When he thought it necessary, he would offer his opinion on a document or attempt to clarify something not quite clear. When it grew very late, the meeting broke up and the men left, all clearly chastened and deeply saddened by what they had read and heard that day.

Chapter Three

In 1944, when news of the Russian invasion into Germany became known and the proximity of defeat ever more imminent, Commandant Werner Hass and his family fled over night from the Schlossberg Concentration Camp by way of the SS Odessa escape route, known as the Ratline, to Argentina. Juan Peron, president of Argentina, had sold ten thousand blank passports to the German Odessa organisation which provided asylum for thousands of German war criminals.

In 1959, Werner Hass and his wife were killed in a car crash whilst driving up a steep hill of a road leading to their house in Buenos Aires in Argentine. A close inspection of the car revealed that somebody had tampered with the brakes. Rumours of the perpetrators who carried out this assassination suggested that repatriated victims from the Schlossberg Concentration camp, a vigilante group, determined to trace German War criminals and inflict their own form of punishment were responsible.

After the death of the Hass parents and having witnessed the atrocities committed by their father when they were still young children, their daughters Gudrun and Erma and their brother Dedrik, by then all over 20 years of age, became scared about their own safety and made plans to return to Europe, for which purpose they had first to sell family property in Argentine. Erma however, said that to escape from the vigilante hunters she was going to the new State of Israel to work on a kibbutz and try to give back to the Jews what people like her father had taken away; maybe even become a Jew, in that way, she would not be suspected.

The following year Gudrun and Dedrik returned to Germany and changed their names from Hass to Hesse. Erma, in Israel, adopted the name of Zimmerman. Erma registered herself as a displaced person; her story was that having lost her parents in the Holocaust, her records, birth details and addresses had all disappeared when her parents were taken away. She said that they had not been put in a concentration camp, but that they had been killed. She said that after the war she was sent to a convent and other places of refuge. She declared herself Jewish and was accepted into Israel. Erma was helped to find a suitable Kibbutz where she could learn the language and have full integration into the country.

In 1962, Erma was finally traced by her brother and sister through messages which she had placed in German newspapers, applying the code word "Lutz 1936 H" which they had selected as a code before they left Argentina. Lutz Lang was a German Olympic athlete in 1936, and the H was for their family name, Hass.

Dedrik, who was then living in Germany, had noticed the code in a German newspaper and had informed Gudrun who was living in Antwerp in Belgium. Gudrun wrote to Erma and arrangements were made to have a family meeting in Paris at a convenient time.

Chapter Four

Mordechai Steinberg died in 1964. His son, Benjamin and daughter Adele, were by then living in the United States of America with their own families. Mrs Steinberg had died just six months earlier and so profound was their love for each other that it was said that Mordechai had died of a broken heart.

Gershon had grown into a wealthy bachelor because of the Steinberg family. They had given him a home, an apprenticeship, a partnership and, more importantly, their love, the love of which from his own family Gershon had been denied. Gershon mourned Mordechai as a son would have mourned his own father. Benjamin and Adele were very well settled in America with a large property portfolio. They offered Gershon the opportunity to take over the company. He refused their generous offer and insisted instead that he be allowed to give them a percentage of all the profits. He emphasised the fact that he could not break ties with a family that had given him a life that he could never have envisaged, a purpose to live and to prosper which he could not otherwise possibly have done. Gershon looked upon himself as part of the Steinberg family and Benjamin and Adele as his brother and sister.

Chapter Five

The world diamond centre in Tel Aviv advertised, within their circle of experts, for competent speakers to visit kibbutzim around the country. They were required not only to demonstrate how diamonds and gemstones could be worn around necks and on arms and fingers but also their many uses in industry. Gershon Marcovitch, a frequent visitor to the diamond centre in Israel, was known for his very popular talks at technical trade schools, where future craftsmen and women were studying lapidary. He was therefore one of the first to be approached to organise group lecture tours around the country.

One late autumn evening he was giving an open-air lecture at the Tel Haifa Kibbutz. Most of the kibbutz residents were sitting on the grass as a gentle breeze coming in from the sea cooled the air.

He always ended his talks with a slot for questions, but on this occasion all the girls present just jokingly asked for free samples. One girl stood out, with her bright blue eyes and her platinum blonde hair, waving her hands in the air and shouting, 'Samples.' He couldn't resist. 'You'll have to marry me first,' he replied. Later that evening, in the kibbutz dining hall, the girl came over and introduced herself simply as

Erma. Gershon offered to get her a drink. They chatted and Gershon was very impressed with Erma. She spoke Spanish, English, German, French and Hebrew. He was told that she was a great asset to the kibbutz community and very popular with its international kibbutz volunteers.

Erma and Gershon were very attracted to each other, and they kept in contact by post and met whenever possible. Their letters became more and more romantic and when they met, they knew they were in love. In October 1964, when the fierce relentless heat of the summer had cooled, Gershon and Erma married in the Tel Haifa kibbutz on a warm, balmy evening with all the residents and volunteers as guests. Erma had informed her sister and brother of her marriage to Gershon but had said nothing about them to him and they were not invited to the wedding. There was still the fear of being identified as the Hass children which might lead to the Schlossberg vigilantes seeking blood revenge.

The new Marcovitch couple settled in Antwerp in Gershon's apartment, in The Royal Leopold Luxury Apartments on the Rue de Liberation. Their marriage was a very happy one, blighted only by the fact that they wanted to have children, but that was not working for them. Erma consulted a gynaecologist, fearing she was infertile. But the result of tests confirmed this was not the case; Gershon was obviously impotent, but Erma did not disclose that to him.

In March 1965 Gershon was in America on business and Erma used that opportunity to contact her sister Gudrun who she asked to meet her in Paris. Erma had always liked Paris, and even when she was on the kibbutz there were excursions once a year for some of the girls to visit fourteen the shops and the fashion shows, so it did not seem strange to Gershon when she told him that she was going to Paris.

Gudrun was puzzled and worried at the urgency of Erma's phone call and quickly made a reservation for both in the George V Hotel on the Avenue George V in Paris. As soon as they were together in the privacy of the hotel's luxurious bedroom, Erma told Gudrun the result of the tests and that although she was very fertile, she would never be able to have a baby with Gershon. The two girls wept in each other's arms. After a while, Gudrun suggested that Erma should have intercourse with Dedrik, her brother, because any child born would look so like Erma, that suspicion could not arise. Erma was persuaded but the plan heralded tragedy.

Chapter Six

Life in Antwerp continued as normal, until one day in June 1966 when Erma ran into Gershon's arms and announced that she was pregnant. Gershon wanted children and had prayed for a miracle and in February 1967 that "miracle" came true when Erma gave birth to twin girls. Just like their mother, the girls had blue eyes and blonde hair.

Although Gershon had a competent staff and a trustworthy manager, Harry Segal, he always liked to be in easy reach of Antwerp and his business. Family holidays were spent in Antibes in the South of France, twice a year. Erma still had her "girly weekends in Paris", purportedly with friends from the kibbutz, and when she did so the children would be booked into a luxury kindergarten. Gershon would visit them frequently to make sure that they were well looked after. Life could not have been more perfect.

It was in June 1970 that Erma decided to take a holiday in Rome for two weeks. Gershon was heavily engaged with overseas customers in Antwerp after which he was due to attend a trade fair in London. Gershon concluded his meetings in Antwerp and should have gone immediately afterward to London but for a last-minute change of venue; he had instead to go to Paris.

Whenever Gershon visited Paris, he had traumatic memories of the time when thousands of Jews were rounded up in 1941 and 1942 and sent to concentration camps, his family amongst them. He had lived as a young child through the screams, the beatings, the hunger the killings, and the slaughter of his own family, it would all come rushing back whenever he came to Paris. He never spoke to anybody about those horrors. When asked about his family and how they had died, he always said that he couldn't remember. But he was haunted by the sight of his family falling dead in front of him as he fled the bullets.

On Sunday, the seventh June, the newly convened meetings in Paris over, Gershon, with some of his business colleagues, went off to take lunch in a restaurant in the Rue De Mail. The restaurant was crowded but Gershon, using his charm and with a little monetary persuasion, managed to achieve a window table. In amiable company, lunch was enjoyable, following which the men relaxed with cigarettes and liberal amounts of brandy in warmed glasses. Gershon settled back happily in his chair by the window and turned to take in and smiled at the busy scene outside.

He was just about to turn away from the window when he saw a man and two women walking arm in arm, laughing and singing as they moved with the crowd, a picture of happiness. All three were very blonde, similar in height and the two women were obviously twin sisters, one of whom was Erma, his wife.

Chapter Seven
Retribution

Gershon gave his apologies to his colleagues and hastily left the restaurant. Without really knowing what he intended to do, he pushed his way through the crowded streets trying not to lose sight of Erma and the other two, oblivious to the complaints of the people that he pushed aside. He followed them to a hotel off the Champ Elysees and watched them go in. He waited a few minutes and, after ensuring that they were not in the reception area, he entered the hotel. He introduced himself to the receptionist as a street fashion photographer and said that he was fascinated by the striking appearance of the three people who had just entered the hotel. The hotel concierge, standing nearby, laughed and said, that they were a family of twin sisters, and their brother and that they stayed in the hotel twice a year. Gershon felt sick and could not get out of the hotel quickly enough. He staggered to the nearest taxi stand with his head spinning like a top he told the driver to take him to the Gare du Nord railway station, but then remembered that he had first to collect his luggage. He had the taxi wait for him whilst he did that and checked out of his hotel. He then completed his journey to the Gare du Nord from where he knew there was a direct train to Antwerp Central station.

Erma was not due back for another week which gave Gershon time to investigate, not only why his wife was in Paris, when she was supposed to be in Rome, but much more importantly, why she had never revealed to him the fact that she had a sister and brother. He feared the reason for her secrecy.

On arriving back home in the Royal Leopold Apartments, Gershon went immediately to their bedroom. Erma had a little desk there and he emptied the drawers and looked through letters and notebooks. He went to Erma's dressing room and without attempting to hide what he was doing, he frenetically emptied all her handbags, checked for letters or diaries, looked in shoeboxes. He began looking in the pockets of clothes hanging in her wardrobes and at the back of one of the wardrobes he found a small leather briefcase, out of sight under a collection of hats. The briefcase was locked and although he tried to force the lock it did not budge. Mordechai had owned a large collection of keys, which he had used to open customers' jewellery boxes, if the original keys had been lost. He had passed those keys to Gershon.

The next day, Gershon had no difficulty in selecting a key to fit the briefcase which he found on opening was crammed with letters. And there was also in the case a key with a label attached to it. The label was printed with the name of a well-known storage company located near to the docks. The label also bore the name Gudrun Hesse. Gershon set the key aside and started to read the letters.

The letters were mainly from Gudrun and Dedrik Hesse. But among them was a letter from the gynaecological department of a private hospital in Paris which had the results of Erma's examination four years previous. He read the report and stood transfixed at the knowledge that Erma was fertile and that the reason why they had not been able to have children when they first married was inevitably because he was impotent. A later letter from Gudrun was even more horrifying for Gershon as it disclosed that Dedrik was the Father of the children, he had been led to believe were his own. There were more letters from Gudrun and Derik after that, but Gershon was too distraught to read more. He fell asleep on the bed and did not wake until the next morning.

It was Monday and Erma was not due home until the following week. Still deeply distressed and burning with curiosity, Gershon washed and dressed quickly then drove to the storage company and presented the label and the key he had found in the briefcase. It took just twenty minutes for the receptionist, using the key Gershon had handed to her, to open a secure locker from which she extracted a small, locked trunk which she handed to Gershon.

At home in his apartment, he carried the trunk to the library to which only he had access. It was his other, secret world. There, in the library, he opened the trunk with a key from his collection. He found himself staring at a framed picture of a German officer with three children at his side: Two little girls and a boy. The picture, in black and white, was unfaded. It was clear to see that this was a family portrait. Everybody in it had very fair hair; the two little girls looked like twins.

Beneath the layer of letters, he saw a zipped clothes cover. It looked quite bulky and when he picked it up it seemed too heavy to contain just a jacket or suit. He took it to his bedroom and placed it on the large, double bed. He undid the zip and screamed; on the bed before him was a German officer's uniform, a Luger handgun and a box of ammunition. On the shoulder epaulettes he saw, embroidered in gold, the initials "SS". In the lining of the jacket, in elaborate letters was the name Werner Hass, a name which struck fear and trembling into Gershon, the name of the commandant of the Schlossberg Concentration Camp. How many times had Gershon seen that gun, was this the same gun in the hand of the man who had killed his father, mother and sisters? That man's jacket and that man's gun were now lying on Gershon and Erma's, bed.

In a state of shock, he stumbled over to his safe and removed the chess board that his father had made in the Schlossberg concentration camp. He ran his hands over the chess board, all that he had left of his family. He caressed the board which his father had made at night in the concentration camp, metaphorically holding his father's hand and touching his fingers, as he carved the chess pieces. He placed the black king on the board to represent Commandant Werner Hass and his family. He then set up an odd checkmate move, comprising the white king, white pawn and white Bishop. The white queen and two white pawns played no part in the checkmate move; but he positioned them where he thought they must be. He bent over and kissed the head of the white king, his father. He kissed the head of the white queen, his mother. He lifted the two white pawns in his hand, held them to his breast and kissed them, his sisters. One lonely white pawn, the executioner, he placed in front of the Hass family. Checkmate. He promised his family he would be with them very soon.

From reading the most recent letters in the trunk, Gershon had found Gudrun's address in Antwerp. He also learnt that when their stay in Paris with Erma came to an end, Dedrik, who still lived in Germany, would come to Antwerp to stay overnight with Gudrun before returning home the following morning. They would all three be back in Antwerp on Monday.

Gershon drove his car through the summer rain, it was Sunday, a warm wet and comforting day, after days of relentless sunshine. Gershon parked his car near to the apartment building where, he had discovered, Gudrun lived. After a short wait, he saw a car pull up outside Gudrun's apartment building and a man and a woman alighted, laden with luggage and entered the building. Both were very fair-haired. He had no difficulty in recognising them, because had it not been for her clothes, he might have thought the woman was Erma. But Erma was not due back until Monday, and Gudrun was, quite obviously, not just Erma's sister, but her twin sister. Satisfied that he had firmly established Gudrun's address and that she and Dedrik were there, he returned to his own apartment.

At 4 am the next day, Monday morning, Gershon returned and sat in his car two buildings away from Gudrun's apartment and waited. Just after 6 am, as he had expected, Dedrik and Gudrun emerged from the apartment building each carrying cases. Dedrik opened the car and placed a case in the boot; Gudrun bent over to assist him with another case. As they both bent over, Gershon approached from behind them. Two shots echoed in the empty street; two bodies slumped to the ground. Gershon drove away.

Erma was expected at 4 pm that same day after collecting the children from their nursery hotel, on her way home from the station. The children rushed laughing at Gershon and hugged him as he welcomed them back home, Erma, threw her arms around his neck and kissed him. He directed them to sit at the dining table. He told them to close their eyes as he had a surprise for them.

Gershon Marcovitch, a quiet and serious man, who loved his wife and the two children he thought were his own, did what he thought he had to do. He took five lives, and in doing so he ended the tainted blood of the Hass family and revenged the Marcovitch family.

Quietly and carefully, Inspector Arnaude Babineaux continued to read Gershon's story, every page describing his life, his feelings, his passions, pain and remorse. He, Babineaux, read the chess board in front of these assembled legal minds like a book, and explained to the shocked but fascinated men how and why Gershon had positioned the chess pieces on the board. With tears in his eyes, he described the meaning of the symbolic farewell that Gershon had made to his family. The lonely white pawn, he told them, was Gershon Marcovitch, the executioner, standing in front of the Hass family.

Babineaux stopped reading the diary, letters and notes, bending his head forward he said, 'Was this murder, or an execution by a good man twenty who, in just two weeks, had lost his reason? And as I said in the beginning, I look to you for guidance and for justice.'

Academia
Educating Gerald

As a child growing up in war time, I attended eleven schools without passing exams, although I did well in woodwork, sports, swimming, boxing, gymnastics, 120-yard-high hurdles, 440-yard obstacle race, fencing and getting the cane. I had no scholarships, no 11 Plus and no O or A levels.

I was evacuated three times, but each time returned home at the wrong time with my mother and sister. Evacuated in 1939 and home in 1940 for the Blitz; evacuated in 1941 and again home in 1943 in time for the rockets. My sister Ruth and I were then evacuated in 1944 to Amersham but returned to London two weeks later as the result of an altercation between a little 10-year-old cockney me, and the rather grand lady of the house. All these movements and my version of Home and Away precluded continuity of education. I harboured ambitions, but I was always conscious of the fact that my lack of education would prevent me from achieving goals I had in mind. I had good and loving parents but their ambitions for me did not exceed their own and, on leaving school aged fifteen, I was sent to work in a clothing factory which I hated. I volunteered for National Service at the earliest possible opportunity and joined the Royal Air Force where, at last, I started on a learning curve.

I was posted to a station for training air crews to convert from piston planes to fly jet bombers, extremely dangerous work. I was not a flier, but I took and passed practical exams in nursing as a medic in Bomber Command. I was involved in rescuing the crews when they crashed or when there was the dreaded "bucket job", as well as practical nursing. I also worked on decompression training, which is taking aircrews up to 40,000 feet in a steel chamber to condition them for high altitude flying.

In the air force I met men who had benefitted from the education I had been denied and with some of them I learnt about music and art and literature, and I began to read. And, as I did so, I became enthralled with history.

For many years, my life revolved around my wife and my children and about earning a living. I suffered a serious illness which took me out of the factory I owned and into a taxi. It was simply not enough for me and in my spare time I studied to become a British Tourist Guide. This was a two-year course, largely based on English history. Getting the famous Blue Badge meant that I could guide people, mostly visitors to the UK, around the places I loved and tell them about the history. I wanted to be the best guide possible, and I was often said to be just that, a source of enormous pride. But it was still not enough for me.

And so, it was, that in 2008, I said to my wife Carole and my sons that I would like to study for a BA in Open University. Before I could finish the sentence, they all said, 'Go for it.' It was Open University that I had in mind mainly because of my lack of basic educational achievement and I applied for their curriculum. However, as a guest at a meeting of my wife's Rotary club I happened to mention my intentions to Sue Jackson, now Professor Sue Jackson, wife of Robert Jackson, a member of Redbridge Rotary club at the time. Sue recommended me to apply to Birkbeck College where I would be a real undergraduate, and experience college life, as opposed to the distance learning in the Open University.

Birkbeck College holds open evening interviews three or four times a year during the midsummer recess, and I attended one at the Royal National Hotel. Interviewers for hundreds of topics were seated at desks filling a great room. When my turn to be interviewed came I was asked why I wanted to study at Birkbeck; my rather naïve answer was that I wanted to prove that Richard III was the rightful King of England. Later, on my way home, I thought that I had made a fool of myself and that it was BA goodbye before I had even started. However, I had been given an application form to fill in with my CV and I think that being a Blue Badge Guide helped somewhat in getting accepted. On Monday 17th March 2009 I passed my Institute of Advance Motoring driving exam at the age of seventy-four, and on Tuesday the 18th of March, I was invited to attend an interview with Professor Hilary Saphire at Birkbeck College. I knocked on her door and as I placed one leg inside, I said, 'Professor Hilary, before I come in, have I been accepted?'

With a smile she said, 'Come in Gerald and sit down.' I was in.

In two days, I had achieved two goals; one to prove that I could still drive properly and the other to be accepted into the University of London.

I bought myself a small pink notebook with an elastic band round it to take notes. My son and daughter-in-law bought me a Mont Blanc pen and a laptop soon followed. In my ignorance, I thought I was properly equipped. Four years later, my flat became too small to hold the books, papers, and the hundreds of ring leaf folders.

My first lecture was an introduction by a Professor on religion and the medieval life of Cathars and Catholics. It took place in a large lecture room and there were about 150 people attending. Sitting beside me was a woman who looked like Margaret Rutherford, who, pointing her finger at my hearing aid shouted at the lecturer, 'Speak up, this man is deaf.' I could have strangled her. At the cheese, wine and snacks gathering after the lecture I heard people, some of whom already had degrees from Oxford and Cambridge, engaged in in-depth analysis of medieval life. I had chosen this subject for my degree course. I did not even know then that I was taking an Honours Degree. My thoughts went back to my 25-yard swimming certificate. I was in another world, and I was afraid; I was very afraid! I was approached by one of the tutors who asked me if I had enjoyed the lecture. He assured me it would get better.

Three weeks into my degree course, I had serious doubts as to my ability to stay at Birkbeck and I made an appointment to see my designated tutor.

The room was, as I imagined it to be, with brown leather armchairs, wall to wall books. My designated tutor was a tall man in a grey double-breasted suit with a mop of grey hair, not exactly Michael Cain, in Educating Rita. I told him that I had doubts about my future at the college and was left in even greater confusion when he said that in his capacity as designated tutor, he only looked to students with family problems and financial problems. I got up and walked out of his room and was prepared to call it a day. As luck would have it my seminar tutor, Lucus Balaminus was emerging from his own office just a few doors down the corridor. I told him my doubts about continuing with the course, to which he said, and I remember very clearly his words. 'If you need to talk to anyone, come to me, because you are going to get your degree.' I cherished his words, and he, and all at Birkbeck, tutors, librarians and all the staff gave me the confidence to continue with the course.

I did not find it easy, but Carole had warned me that it would require extreme dedication and sacrifices. I continued my work as a taxi driver/British Tourist Guide throughout the four years. I studied on average eight hours a day and read volumes of books and wrote many thousands of words. In four years at college, I never missed a lecture, never missed a deadline, presented my essays, and gave verbal presentations every term. I was the oldest student in my year, but I made many friends and my fellow students, and I comforted each other, particularly in the bar after lectures. We were not drunk with drink; we were drunk with knowledge that we had absorbed through research and lectures. We shared notes and sent emails with advice on which site to visit and download on the computer. Whenever we were presented with lists of essay choices or when there were doubts about choosing a subject for a dissertation there was feverish communication amongst us. In addition to our lectures, we had one-to-one tutorial, which were like confessionals where we were able to establish a great rapport with our lecturers who helped us to decide which topic would best suit the individual student.

Each year when revising for an exam my whole being became traumatised by questions such as how many modules should I revise?

I established a modus operandi; I knew I would be asked three out of perhaps ten or fifteen questions, some of which would be in three or four parts. I concentrated on about six main topics and wrote copious notes on those; the little pink notebook long having been abandoned for the purpose. Not to answer one question was a failure, no matter how well one had done in the others. The relief on completing a three-hour exam was palpable and fully exhibited in the college bar. If the sun shone, we would gather on the terrace and indulge in revisiting the questions and discussing our approach and answers.

Waiting for the results was, perhaps, the hardest part for the whole family. They were always supportive and optimistic, but we would all have been satisfied if I had scraped through with a third. Somehow, I managed to pass every paper in every exam culminating in my attaining a 2.2 BA Honours degree in history. I had achieved the ambition that, for most of my life, I had hardly dared to express, even to myself. I loved every day of those four years, hard yes, extremely hard, but infinitely worth it.

And then the great day arrived, and we were to attend the graduation ceremony. I had, to my utter astonishment, received a letter saying that I was the joint winner of the Daikin Prize, of which I had never previously heard, and I received a cheque for £100. The real benefit, I thought, was that it allowed me to have more than the usual two guests for the ceremony. So, we invited my younger son and daughter-in-law, my sister and Carole's sister, an overseas friend and

Carole, of course. But she, wicked woman, acquired another ticket and, in well-kept secrecy, my elder son who lives in New Zealand arrived a few days before the great day. And they were all there, with the lovely Professor Sue Jackson beaming on the dais with all the other professors and dignitaries, to hear that I had received the Daikin Prize for being the Birkbeck student of the year. I fell up the steps when I went up to receive my certificate, but I was already on top of the world. I had my education; I was Gerald Nathanson, BA (Hons). I was somebody.

By the Waters of Stepney Green

SET IN THE EARLY 1950s

Chapter One

The billowing November fog outside the waiting room of Dr Rabin's surgery was ignorant of the frustration and anger which permeated the air of this tightly packed, stuffy and smelly room. The smell from the spluttering paraffin heater in the corner of the waiting room mingled with the taste of the thick green as pea soup fog, which whirled and twirled, whispering beneath the surgery waiting room door. Patients, mostly elderly, a number smoking, added to this accumulated fug.

The walls of the surgery were once bright yellow and brown. That is, they were, when Dr Rabin set up his medical practice six years earlier. Today it is light and dark brown, caused by the cigarettes smoked by the patients, and by the damp foggy weather.

The winter club had begun, elderly people, sitting in rows on benches waiting for their weekly dose of tonics and pills, medicine that will steer them through the winter months until the warm, clear spring days herald in a hopeful healthier body. As each patient went in to see the doctor a space on the bench was created, the rest of the patients then shuffled along the form in unison, except for those who sat snug around the solitary heater on individual hard backed and hard-seated chairs.

This doctor's waiting room, to these several old people, was an operation's room, where they planned argued and commiserated with one another. This day, more than any other, was the beginning and the end of a schemed plan. 'Awl right,' said one of them, Percy Armitage. 'Let's awl get togever and do somfin. I for one will not be seen dead in that bloody old work'ouse. That's wot it is, a bloody work'ouse.' He stood up and sat down repeatedly, agitation showing in his every movement. He was a big man, weighing about seventeen stone, (238 lbs) his cronies called him 'all mouth and trousers', not only for his size but because his large frame was draped with a pair of enormous trousers, a 'belt and braces man', the belt disappearing into the folds of fat which encircled his belly. As well as being big, the other great feature of Percy was his obstinacy. He was honest and outspoken, and often aired his opinions loudly and at length on any subject whether it was one with which he was acquainted or not. He had acquired a certain reputation amongst his fellow old age pensioners of Stepney Green, as being, in some respects, a leader. And on this crucial day in Dr Rabin's surgery, they looked to him to voice their grievances, as chairman, a representative, to confront authority. Groups of old people all over Stepney Green's East End of London huddled together, pooling their fading strength to protect their remaining years, often meeting in the waiting rooms of doctors' surgeries, and pensioners' clubs. For once, Percy Armitage was holding forth on a subject which he really understood, and out of which he intended to derive some pleasure from the experience by broadcasting his opinions.

But he was interrupted by a voice from the corner of the room near to the smelly spluttering and totally ineffective heater. 'I didn't catch your name, Mr...err?' 'Armitage,' said Percy, annoyed by the interruption and about to proceed when again, 'I don't know your first name Mr Armitage.' The voice insisted upon an answer.

His false teeth, never being properly seated in his mouth, were pushed from one side to the other, as if he were chewing a wad of tobacco.

He hissed out "Purrcee", sheepishly, hating to admit to it, as all his acquaintances had only ever known him by his nickname, "all Mouth and Trousers or 'Old Army. He had always been accepted by it and never needed to divulge his hated first name, he thought it was not manly enough for him.

'Weel,' in a high-pitched squeal, again from the voice of Emily Randle. who was seated near to the oil stove in the corner of the waiting room.

'I think that Mr Armitage is quite right, and that we should consummate our ideas.'

'Wot's she says?' said a frail Alfie White, lifting his red nose above the pages of the Sporting Life newspaper, firm in the knowledge that the Bookies and their runners wouldn't earn a fortune out of Alfie's meagre pension.

'Oh! Don't worry abaht er, she's clever, she is,' answered his neighbour, seated beside him on the hard wooden bench. 'Er! Farver, is the one, wot was the gardener to that big noise Lord Chaney, when 'e lived in the big 'ouse near the 'orspital 'e wos.'

The face belonging to the voice delivering Emily Randel's curriculum vitae, was unshaven, toothless and slobbering. The sound of quietness descended over the waiting room, the body attached to the voice preened itself for delivering such knowledge, such wonderful gossipy knowledge.

Our new celebrity in the waiting room likewise stretched herself in a similar manner. She was not just a gardener's daughter. Mrs Randle, in her own way regarded her connection with Lord Chaney, no matter how distant from royalty, as aristocracy, and was pleased that it had elevated her standing in the waiting room, a point made perfectly clear without her digging, into her past.

Emily Randle was a hypochondriac, as well as an inverted snob. She regularly took laxatives, to relieve her congested system, and the words she spouted, however misused, was very much in the vein of Lady Malaprop, but to Emily, it gave her, as she thought, an air of gentility. As she was about to continue, Dr Rabin entered the waiting room to begin his morning surgery. 'The only consummation round here will take place between you,' and he pointed to Percy, 'and you.' As he pointed to Emily. The patients erupted into raucous laughter. He paused to collect his morning mail, which had been opened and sorted by Lily, his receptionist. She sat behind a door with one panel removed to make a hatch, leading to a small room where the patients 'files were stored in two old, second hand, dark brown wooden cabinets.

In her cockney brogue, Lily brought compassion and warmth into the dreary waiting room. Sifting through the post was her daily chore, medical journals, samples and advertisements, putting to one side letters that required urgent attention from the doctor. They both entered the surgery laden with the post, Lily handing to him the most important of the morning mail. In this quiet time, before the patients entered the surgery, Pilip, the doctor, and his faithful woman

"'Woman Friday" Lily, spent the few minutes allotted to them in having a cup of coffee, and by him, the doctor, complaining about his problems, either at home or in the surgery.

'I'm nod well, Lily,' he said, 'nod well ad all.' His diction this morning was very nasal and difficult to understand, owing to his cold but to Lily it was the sound of a BBC announcer; she adored him. "Aahtishoo!" The sound and the blast of his explosive sneeze reverberated off the walls of the surgery.

To be truthful, he wasn't well at all. 'Make an appoindment for me do see a specialist at the London Hospital,' he said, dabbing his nose with a large handkerchief taken from his coat pocket.

'When shall I make it for? Tomorrow?' she asked.

He considered and said, 'No, not tomorrow. I'm playing a round of golf with Gilbert, the chemist from across the road.'

'Wednesday?'

'No, there's a Rotary dinner that can't be missed.'

'Thursday then?'

He consulted his dairy. 'No, 'fraid not, I'm attending a lecture on hygiene in the home and cleanliness in hospitals.' He sneezed spreading droplets all over his desk. In desperation she suggested Friday, to which he laughed, and said, 'Christ lily, by then I'll probably be better.'

'Right,' she said.

'Overture for beginners, let's get the show on the road, send in the first victim in five minutes.' Lily walked out of the surgery into her action quarters and prepared for the daily dosage of pills, tonics, creams and sympathy. She knew most of the patients by their first name and prepared the cards with their details on it and certificates for the regulars, the pill and potion brigade.

Philip stood before the mirror near to his overstocked instrument cupboard, combed his ruffled greying black hair, took a bottle from his medicine cabinet and emptied some of the contents into a glass and gargled. He then took a pill chosen from the assortment of samples on his desk, then inhaled deeply from an inhaler which emerged with another a large linen handkerchief out of his coat pocket. Having removed his greatcoat, he stood ready for the day's work in a grey tweed jacket smelling softly of mothballs, and strongly of disinfectant. Dr Rabin pressed his buzzer which activated a light in the waiting room over Lily's head and summoned the patients into his surgery. She handed a card to Mrs Greenbaum, one of her special favourites, who had been sitting quietly during the pre-surgery debate. Mr Malka Greenbaum was small, round and balanced on tiny feet which were encased in shabby fur-lined boots, bought second hand in a used clothes shop in Whitechapel High Street, like everything else she wore. Her eyes were small and close set; a Semitic nose and high cheek bones underlined her Eastern European Origins. Although she had lived in England since childhood, and loved the country passionately, she retained a strong Eastern European accent, and only wrote in Yiddish.

'Gutt mornink dokatur,' she said in a most determined manner. From her voice, and the way the greeting to the doctor, Philip Rabin knew that Mrs Greenbaum's troubles were not entirely medical, in the sense that she was not physically ill. She gave him a feeling of guilt because she asked very little of life, and he, like everyone else demanded so much more. There had been times when he had thought his needs were more important than those of others. But now Philip knew better. Mrs Greenbaum lowered herself slowly onto the edge of the chair which faced the doctor, bending forward over the consulting deska jumble of papers, pill boxes, a stethoscope and various medical paraphernalia, her body now part of the table's confusion.

'What can I do for you?' asked Philip.

'You see, dokatur,' said Mrs Greenbaum. 'It's mein head.'

'You have a pain in your head?' asked Philip, who was now lifting himself slowly out of his chair.

'No, I 'av a vorry in mein head, in my 'eart I avve the pain.' Philip was now standing beside Malka, aware of her misery and pain, and conscious of the worries of all his elderly patients now sitting in the crowded stuffy waiting room. She continued talking as if Philip wasn't there. 'All mein life I 'av vorked for mein 'usband and mein kinder (children). I scrubbed floors and cooked, and if mein kinder vere ill I felt their pain. The only pleasure I ever had in life is my little room vis all mine bits and pieces, and now dokatur, mine kinder vant to put me into aah vorkouse.' Her hands were aged and wrinkled, but clean and delicate, it's aged skin, still beautifully formed, worked the catch on her handbag open and shut, the clicking of the catch the only other sound in the room. 'I vent vitout food, vitout shoes in mine feet.' She started to sob and broke into Yiddish, the better to express her poor hurt feelings. Philip had heard Yiddish spoken in his own home as a child, but he had never mastered it, except for a few words and even fewer expletives. Because of that he understood very little of what Malka was saying. He had to calm the old lady if he were to help her, indeed, he would have

55

to calm them all that morning, to reassure the congregation that had gathered in his waiting room, but none more so than Mrs Greenbaum. All of them were afraid of leaving their old familiar dwellings, but Philip thought that Malka would find it hardest of all to adjust to the move. The old woman had enough intelligence to realise that she wouldn't survive the changes taking place. The East End, nearly razed to the ground by the German bombs, was being rebuilt. Stepney Green was falling, it was being subjected to a major post war redevelopment scheme. The young married couples with children would be given flats in tower blocks, with fitted kitchens and central heating, a luxury never seen before in the depressed East End.

The children could abandon the streets and play in the green areas, swing on the swings, slide on the slides, or go dizzy on the roundabout. Only the old folks would be left to regret and resent the unstoppable change. Some, the lucky ones, would be joining their children in maisonettes, or sharing flats with spinster daughters, perhaps.

But many were clinging pitifully to the old rundown dwellings, because the alternative was the dreaded old people's home, dreaded by the memories of what it used to be, a Victorian workhouse. The same building that Percy Armitage was committed against, and Malka Greenbaum feared like the tomb. All hated it because it would deprive them of their privacy and most of all their pride. London's East Enders were a very proud people.

Earlier that morning before he had left his house, Philip had received an impassioned telephone call from Gertie Freed, the daughter of Malka, and the elder of her three children. She had urged the doctor to certify her mother physically fit to enter the "workhouse", otherwise she would be obliged to have her mother come to live with her in her flat. 'Of cause Phil,' she said, presuming on the fact that at one time they had attended the same school. 'Of cause, you know I want Mummy, but I have a young daughter and Mummy, bless her, has habits I don't have to tell you, who knows better than you.'

Philip extracted a paper tissue from the box on his desk, sniffed deeply with his inhaler and cast his mind back. He had no difficulty in recalling Gertie Greenbaum, now Freed, and her daughter, because both bore a strong resemblance to Malka, the mother and grandmother. But Gertie's features were sharpened by greed and selfishness, so that in place of her mother's pleasant oriental appearance, her's were florid and fat, a reflection of her overindulgence and sloth-like life. Philip Rabin knew that Gertie and her two brothers would not like to be reminded of their mother's personal sacrifices for them. He had met Gertie's brothers on one occasion when paying a home call and realised that there was little hope of help from that direction if it were needed. Malka had to be calmed down and he thought that he knew the way to do it. 'Mrs Greenbaum,' he said, assuming his most comforting demeanour, his sneezing bout over, and his head consumed with the welfare of the woman in front of him not of the cold which seemed to ease with the silent plea for help from Malka. 'My dear woman, why are you upsetting yourself like this, there is really no cause for all this alarm.' The quiet confidence in his voice stopped her harsh sobs. He continued saying, 'None of my patients will go into that disgusting building, I will not allow this thing to happen. You, my dear, are not alone. Outside...' – he pointed to the door leading to the waiting room – 'outside this room, there are many worried people who do not like the idea any more than you do. People in high places, with influence are as aggrieved of the move as we are, and it is hoped that they will help with the plans that we have suggested, the alternative plans for the senior citizens. That building was condemned years ago.'

The building referred to in this conversation was a workhouse built in the time of Queen Victoria, its main function to take poor people and vagrants off the streets and employ them in menial tasks to pay for their food and lodging. In the first world war it had been used as a hospital for the wounded soldiers.

A once red brick structure of the solid Victorian period, now a dark soot-stained demonic building, weeds growing through the walls and surrounded by ugly iron railings, its appearance was that of an old forbidding prison with broken windows caused by the blitz on London, as well as stones thrown by young scallywags. This was what was intended to be converted into an old people's home, and the old people were loathe to enter that unhappy and sad block of bad memories. The Council, after the war, had many demands for accommodation laid at their doors, emergency houses were being erected, prefabricated houses, called pre-fabs, for families. The elders of the community were low down on their list for housing, and the only concession for them was the old building. 'Now understand me and listen to me,' Philip said as he paced around his surgery arms punching the air accentuating his passionate feelings for his patients, and their heart felt anxieties for their future. 'There is nothing wrong with old people living together in the right surroundings, and with people to help and look after them.'

Malka watched the doctor as he marched up and down the surgery gesticulating with his arms to emphasise a point. 'But that place never – **NEVER.**' The never sounding like Winston Churchill during one of his inspirational war time speeches. He turned and faced Malka, the face she saw was moist with sweat, no doubt from his cold, but more likely from his impassioned oration. 'I have appointments to see the Mayor of Stepney Green, the borough surveyor, the welfare officer, the chief housing officer, in fact the whole bloody lot.' He continued, 'Mrs Greenbaum, an old peoples home there must be, and will be, But I will fight to see that none of my elderly patients are moved out of their homes because of the new developments for other people, or for any other reason until the old workhouse is pulled down and a beautiful new building put up in its place.'

Malka was quiet now, she had sat and listened, and at every pause that Philip made she nodded her head and clucked her lips, sounds made by her to show that she approved by muttering, "nyeh". She knew that even Philip Rabin didn't grasp the full extent of her worries, at least in her eyes he was sincere and a very good man. 'You aarh an nanegel, dat's vaht you aarh dokutar, God should be gutt to your family.' She smiled through her tears and prepared to leave the surgery, having regained a little comfort from the knowledge that there was a shoulder on which she could lean on, an ear that would listen. Like many of the doctor's other patients that morning she left feeling better than when she went in, although no pills or medicine had been prescribed.

Chapter Two

Malka's street was among the first which was destined for re-development, now it consisted of ten maisonettes and fifteen terraced houses comprising a parlour and kitchen on the ground floor, a steep narrow staircase climbing up to two bedrooms. There were no bathrooms in these (two up and two down) houses, no inside toilet, and not all had hot water laid on. Outside in the mean sooty backyard which one had to cross in foul weather or fine, was the lavatory and coal bunker, a number of the elderly and the very young in cold weather still used the chamber pot known to all that used one as the Po, conveniently stashed beneath the bed. The close proximity in which these people lived gave rise at times to friction amongst the neighbours, and surely a number of lives were shortened by the damp and cold lack of comforts. And yet, in a crisis, such as the bombing during the blitz they showed a remarkable feeling of camaraderie. The older inhabitants were deeply attached to these poor surroundings, having seen their families born and grow up there, watched their relatives die there, and wished for nothing else than to spend the rest of their lives there. But this was not to be, because progress demanded that they must have what other people thought best for them, and if their requirements did not merit one of the shiny new apartments in the tower blocks it was the old people's home or nothing.

For a time during the Second World War the old building enjoyed a somewhat happier period when it was used as a canteen for those engaged as Air Raid Wardens, Firemen and Fire Watchers, after which it once again become a building of ridicule and abuse. The ever-increasing pressures of overcrowding caused by the lack of housing accomodation, the legacy of six years of war, had caused suggestions to be put forward at council meetings that the old Victorian building should once more be altered to accommodate the old folk. It was only ever intended as a temporary measure, but schools, hospitals, roads and more roads had been given priority over the "Brick Red Monster", and it still stood, in the same state, where it has stood for more than a hundred and fifty years. Dr Philip Rabin, on behalf of the senior citizens on his medical panel, was campaigning to have it demolished, pulled down and replaced by something more suitable and agreeable to old people. Progress was slow, and as the bulldozers closed in the old became frightened of being too old and the project too late.

In the back bedroom of number 28 Marbley Street, Emily Randle sat huddled in her uncut moquette armchair, which, together with a single bed and dark oak wardrobe filled the room overlooking the backyard. Autumn had passed and there was no heating in the room. Emily hugged herself, and pressed her thin frame into the depths of the chair, not because she was cold, but because downstairs her son Neil was having yet another argument with his wife Margaret. And, bitterly, she realised that she, Emily, was the bone of contention. Emily only had one child, Neil, and he was something of a miracle. Nobody had ever seen his father; the neighbours having disposed of him in various different ways. In fact, he had left Emily the morning after their wedding night, having found his bride frigid and unresponsive. No premarital experiments, no passionate embraces as a prelude to marital bliss. Just two very cold virginal people each expecting heaven but instead receiving hell. That Mr Randle, would hardly have believed it if somebody had told him that that agonised and frustrated night had produced a Neil Randle. Perhaps if Mr Randle had been more patient with Emily and kinder in their marital bed, instead of attacking her virginity, so aggressively, they might have had a life together. Instead, it made Emily a priggish hypochondriac, and that is the image that everybody knew her by. Because of that dreadful experience with Neal's father, her attitude towards sex was a standing joke in the dress factory where she worked, hard and well as a forelady, now getting ready for retirement. The staff at Roman Textiles, where Emily worked, were typical of a time when the roar of machinery was reduced whilst the finishing of garments was completed largely by hand, and all listened to Woman's Hour on the radio. The attention of most of the staff, men and women, was captured by a new subject, contraception, a new, quickly recognised as being of much importance. But a voice attempting to sing the Anniversary Waltz suddenly interrupted the programme. It was Emily, red in face, trying hard to pretend that the radio's subject didn't exist and acting as if it were switched off. After that the girls in the factory all agreed that Neil was a child of virgin birth while others thought otherwise, and if right might have made Mr Randle come rushing back to his rejected bride.

On his wage as a bank clerk, Neil supported his wife, Margaret, and his two young daughters, Sheila and Pauline. At the same time, he boosted his mother's income by assisting in paying part of the bill for rent, gas, electricity and coal. Emily had always kept a tight rein on her out goings and never incurred unnecessary debts. Her independence was, since becoming a single mother after her one day of marriage, a way of life. Her son knew that his mother was fully capable of earning her own living and not a financial burden to him or his wife Margaret. But Margaret was pregnant for the third time and in the little terraced house the lack of pace was a real problem. She confronted Neil. Her hair was twisted into a forest of curlers, her eyes were made owl-like by large glasses and her untidy completed the scene.

She was not endowed with tact, diplomacy, or for that matter any feelings of love or passion. Her children had been conceived with an air of quiet resolution. Lying on her back she suffered Neil's unromantic sexual thrusting, by spending the time decorating an imaginary house, and thinking of ways of persuading him to make his mother move into the old peoples' home when she retired from the factor. She told herself that, after all, her mother-in-law was working well beyond her retirement age. Margaret's body moved up and down the bed in rhythm with Neil's sexual exertions, until her head was bouncing off the headboard. 'Enough, Neil' she shouted above his moans.

'Neil, you're hurting me.' Without taking a breath Margaret continued as if nothing had happened and ignoring her husband's panting, continued,

'We'll still be in this house when baby comes, and you know what a (bad time I have in my confinements.'

'She's, meaning Emily) has had a child of her own.' 'She should know that at these times a woman needs a bit of peace and quiet and privacy. You've got to tell her, Neil.'

Draping himself in his blue towelling beach robe, a reminder of a rain-swept holiday in Eastbourne the previous year, and oblivious to his sweaty, wet lovemaking moments before, Neil looked troubled. He sat down on the corner of the bed, his feet searching for his soft tweed slippers with sponge rubber soles, and he rested his head on his hands, elbows on his knees, looking at his feet he said, 'Honestly, Mag, you must remember, that this is her house anyway, and she used to think the world of it when I was a kid, and the neighbourhood had a bit of class.'

'Mum never ever forgot that Lord Chaney came here to pay his respects when Grandad died.' Ignoring this interruption, Margaret just continued. 'And another thing, Sheila and Pauline are getting big girls now, and what with another on the way, well! We just can't have three kids in our room, I could never have a soul in for a cup of tea if any of them had to sleep in the parlour.'

In the next room, Emily by now in her uniform curlers, flannel night dress and tartan dressing gown, had just placed her dentures into a glass beside the bed. Over her head she tied a hair net, all the time trying to close her ears to the conversation coming from the next room. The partitions between the rooms in this house, as in the others in the street, were built of lathe and plaster, and the slightest sound carried through from one room to another.

Emily heard everything that was said in the other room. She sat down and sighed. She had always supported Neil during his upbringing, then bailed him out of irresponsible, unsuccessful business ventures. But now he was employed in a bank and this attack on her by Margaret was too much to bear.

The question of the old people's home, and the rebuilding of it to house the senior citizens of Stepney Green, was now pre-eminent in the minds of those in a similar situation as Emily. She was never afraid of a just fight and was determined to fight for the rights of the aged, she herself coming up to the time when she too would like to retire as she had worked all of her life. Neil. she thought, and his wife, might just be persuaded to assist in the gathering wave of objections to the Council's neglect of the elderly, and mighty be prepared to attend one of the many public meetings in favour of rebuilding of the home.

Chapter Three

At the Armitage house, Percy switched on the television, sat down in his favourite armchair, the springs of which were attempting to push through the well-worn leather seat covering, and relaxed opposite the screen. He rolled himself a cigarette with great precision born out of many years of practise. Slowly, he brought out from his pocket a scratched tin box of Old Holborn Tobacco, placing it on the small rounded metal table between him and the television set. He tapped the lid of the tin, spat on his fingers, pushed open the tin of tobacco with his nicotine-stained fingers and placed the lid under the box. His nose twitched at the smell of the tobacco leaves which he fondly rubbed between his fingers and reduced into a fine grain. Drawing a Rizla cigarette paper out of its packet, he proceeded to fill it with just the right amount of tobacco, sprinkling it carefully along the thin fine paper, his tongue licking the edge gently, his fingers rolling softly along its length. A tap on the table on one end of the homemade cigarette, a tap on the box with the other end, a final twirl of this paper tube, and a sigh of affection as he replaced the lid of the tin and lit up the cigarette. The ritual never varied, and never failed to give Percy pleasure, as he relaxed in the depth of the armchair. He neither cared nor wanted to care, that Dr Rabin insisted that his sometime coughing was caused by inhaling nicotine, or that it was getting expensive to buy, particularly when one lived on a small pension. Percy refused to listen, and the doctor's advice fell on deaf ears. Often having been told to spend more money on nutritious food, and cut down on smoking, Percy would deliberately make himself an extra smoke instead. He was, until recently, contented enough with life, but now things weren't too good at home.

Percy relaxed deeper into the armchair and watched a chat programme, which absorbed all his attention. His reverie was suddenly interrupted in the form of his teenage grandson, Julian. Without so much as a "by your leave", Julian "bopped" into the room and promptly switched over the channel to see a programme of pop tunes, aimed at the teenage population. The rock music echoed around the room, bouncing off the flying geese mounted on the flocked wallpaper. 'Wot the bleeding' 'ell do you think you're doing?' Percy leapt from the comfort of his chair, launched himself across the room, his 'Hay,' said Percy, 'I'm watching that.' And with a theatrical movement, made much of switching the television back to its original station. He resumed his position again in the armchair, and delighted himself in watching a well-known but unpopular politician, being made to squirm by an interviewer who specialised in in-depth questioning on the subject of political chicanery. Not five minutes had elapsed before bedlam again broke out in the form of his daughter Sibyl bursting through the door shouting, 'Honestly, Dad, you disgust me. How can you behave like that, your own grandson, shouting and swearing, honestly.'

'He may be my grandson, but thank Gawd 'e's not my son,' said Percy, once more rising out of his seat, this time pulling up his worn braces which had been resting at his side. 'Look at 'im, Go'rn look at ''im!' 'air daarn to 'is shoulders, a bleeding floral shirt and beads, a bleeding poofter.' Well, that did it. Sibyl began to jump up and down with rage, her lacquered beehive hairdo rocking backwards and forwards as she cursed and swore, and defended her rights, and the rights of her son, Julian, to live their lives in their own way. If he, Percy, wanted to go on living under the same roof as them, he'd just have to realise what he will have to do, that is accept that it was her house and not his, as she now paid the rent. It hurt Percy, and to avoid her tirade he stormed out of the house slamming the door behind him.

It was Saturday, and the day for Percy's weekly bath. Now that the first rush for a bath was over, Percy would have a little longer to lie in the warm water and relax his big frame. Although the main rush of the day had disappeared, there was still a queue of people waiting to go in, but Percy was in no frame of mind to be patient and queue with the rest of the public. He pushed his way through to the ticket office, barging the people out of the way, ignoring the moans and the groans which were aimed at his large pushy body. He steamrolled his way to the peroxide blonde ensconced on a high stool behind the glass partition, which had a half circular hole cut into the glass to pass money through. 'Usual, Nellie,' he said, while passing his money through the partition. Nellie, the peroxide blonde, the roots of her hair now showing strings of the original colour, black, pushed a brass button in the ticket dispenser with one hand, at the same time, with the other, pushing over to Percy a towel and a small bar of hard, yellow soap.

The public bath house was rather more like a club than a place for a person to conduct their ablutions. The amenities or lack amenities, of workmen's houses, the 'two up, two down' dwellings, meant that, unless by virtue of a special grant, or a win on the football pools, a bath and all its accompanying plumbing was unaffordable for the people of Stepney Green. Therefore, it was a necessity, if one wanted to keep clean, to make use of the public baths, usually housed in the same building as a swimming pool and steam room. Obviously, one tended to take one's weekly dip at the same time on the same day of the week, or every two weeks, depending on the fastidiousness of the person concerned. The regularity of these visits turned the bath house into a social club and Percy, who had been attending for over thirty years, was a founder member.

The attendant at the baths was a very important man, because in his hands and his hands alone, lay the entire responsibility of filling the individual baths with water. Jubilation Street Public Baths was an Art Deco styled building, with rounded long narrow mottled panelled glass which interrupted the expanse of polished grey green walls. Payment was made at a large grey green tiled window in return for which tickets, soap and towels were issued. 'Usual, Nellie,' he said. Ten marble stairs led to the entrance hall with its mosaic floor depicting Neptune and his Maidens rising out of the boiling seas. There were other scenes from Greek mythology, Temples, Gods and Goddesses of Herculean proportions, from floor to ceiling. The smell of chlorine, the warmth of the steam rooms and the general feeling of cleanliness permeated the building. The planners and the builders could not have conceived that working men and women were intelligent enough to fill their own baths with water, and so the taps or levers were situated outside each cubicle. When the bather was ready the attendant would fill the bath to the depth and to the temperature, he thought fitting and suitably economical. And if this proved not to be to the satisfaction of the bather, he, or she, had only to shout for more hot or cold water, and if they were lucky, the attendant would then make the adjustment from outside the cubicle.

And it was into this mausoleum that a rather angry Percy entered. He lay back in the warm water, found it to his liking, and before settling down to the more serious business of washing, cast his mind back. He thought of his wife Alice, killed in the Blitz, during the war, he remembered his daughter as a young girl in pigtails, and the good times that the three of them had together rowing boats on the River Lea, Percy's shirt sleeves rolled up, his muscles straining on the oars, picnics in Epping Forest on fine summer days, and afternoon teas in Lyons Corner House, Marble Arch on special occasions. 'Hot water number 9' Fred the attendant, shambled along the wooden duck boards and turned on the tap outside number 9 cubicle. 'Okay, that's enough.' Fred turned off the tap. A bunch of local rowdies arrived, brave in their numbers. Old Fred quaked at the sight of these swaggering young men, soon to be conscripted into the armed services, but, as yet undisciplined "yahoo's". This lot seemed in good humour and didn't try to upset the pile of towels which were stacked on a wooden bench in the corridor or push open any of the cubicle doors, as they were wont to do. Apart from their singing, all appeared safe and under control. 'Hot water number 7' a voice shouted, and Fred ambled to the tap outside number 7 cubicle and turned on the hot water tap. Percy, his thoughts lost in the past was oblivious to the shouts of water for 7 cubicle, until, that is, he was suddenly subjected to a surge of scalding hot water pouring into his bath. His bulk prevented a hasty retreat, his screams of abuse at Fred, and his demands for an immediate turn on of cold water to his bath was interspersed with; 'Wot,' he stammered. 'Wot stupid bleeder said to putot water in my bath? Come on where is 'e, I'll kill the bastard, so 'elp me. I'll ring 'is bloody neck.'

Shouting. jigging up and down in naked agony, he held his red raw scalded testicles tenderly. 'Sorry Army,' said Fred, trying not to look at Percy's very red bulk shaking like a large jelly. 'I thought I 'eared you call 'aaht, 'ot water number 7.

'It wasn't me yah great git,' ranted Percy, his temper now cooling down sufficiently to realise that he was running around with no clothes on. He hastily retreated into his cubicle. Altogether it had not been a good day for Percy. So far, there had been trouble with his grandson, the row with his daughter, and now he had his tender parts scalded. He dressed himself, and grumbling under his breath, set off for the Old Peoples Club, walking with difficulty, his legs wide apart, to give some ease to the area between his legs, hoping that the cool air might penetrate up his trousers to his groin and ease the heat of his scalded testicles.

Tension between the elderly and their children spiralled to areas of bitterness, as well as periods of silence. Neither one talking directly to the other, conversation being transmitted through the grandchildren who delighted in being the heralds of good, or as it transpired on most occasions, bad news.

Emily Randle noticed the depressed expressions on the faces of the elderly during these in-house battles of the families, young and old. Walking through the streets to and from the factory where she worked, the sound of anguish and pain echoed through the walls of the small houses and into her own distraught body. With determination she therefore held a council meeting with her son Neil and her daughter-in-law Margaret. After much persuasion from his mother, and nagging from his wife, who was looking to the future possession of the house, Neil went to the Old Peoples Club to address them on the matter of their welfare, and accommodation for them in their later years.

Emily sat in the audience, old and young together. She admired her son as he spoke about the intended Home and what he would like to see done to improve the welfare of the aged. The young married couples saw this as a last glimmer of light in their quest to take over their parents rented houses, having to share a bedroom with their children would soon be no more. The years of yearning for space, and the non-interference from their mums and dads was drawing near.

Never had the dining hall, normally used for talks and entertainment in the Senior Citizens Club been so crowded. That glimmer of light seen by the young set would, in time, turn into a very dark dismal future, but for now it was an opportunity for the young married couples to show solidarity with their parents, who had been persuaded to go into the "home for the aged" under certain conditions, the most important of which was the rebuilding of the old people's home, a project to which the local council was opposed , as it would cost too much money. By an overall majority, in a vote taken at the Old Peoples Club, it was agreed to make an organised protest against the council and its members. A date for a march for the purpose was made, to take place a few weeks later.

The designated day for the march arrived, a cold damp Sunday in November, the sound of the rain blotted out by the tramp, tramp, tramp of feet belonging to the hundreds of people demonstrating, and chanting, 'Down with the Workhouse, Up with a Home for the Senior Citizens.' It sounded better than calling the old people what they were, old people.

Balloons, buntings, pushchairs with babies wrapped up warm against a cold November morning, rowdy young men armed with broken bricks ready to heave at the old workhouse, now called "Trebovoir Green Old Peoples' Home". Rusty railings, broken windows, dirty fog-blackened brick walls, paths overgrown with weeds. As the march passed the building it roused passionate feelings of discontent amongst the young men, who had some notion as to their grandparent's reluctance to live in that onetime workhouse, and they let loose with an assortment of bricks and milk bottles, some even trying to pull down the railings surrounding the building. In an attempt to keep the march orderly, a sturdy policeman was employed to administer instant justice, by giving a quick flick around the ears to anyone that caught showing practical hostility against the building.

Tower Hill, the seat of many demonstrations over the centuries was, that day, host to a local dispute. After assembling in front of a dais made up of discarded doors from the bomb-damaged houses, milk crates and a variety of other debris found locally, the crowd listened to impassioned speeches. The fiery oratory was delivered from the heart and the soul of the most interested present that day. But two hours of standing in the cold November climate, was enough for many, and boredom was setting in. Dr Philip Rabin, frightened that the first thrust against the indifferent council might melt away, pushed his way to the front of the mob, and climbed the rickety steps leading to the stage.

'People,' he shouted, 'my patients, my very dear friends and supporters.' The fidgeting subsided, the coughing and spluttering ceased. 'We, that is you and I, are dealing with little men, bureaucratic parasites whose only concern in life is for their own greedy growth in wealth.' Philip paused as the crowd shuffled closer shouting, 'Yeh! Yeh!' Raising his arms to quieten them he continued. 'They don't give a damn if you have a home to move into or not, if you live in overcrowded circumstances or not.' You could reach out and feel the silence, the cold ignored, every eye centred on Philip's face, his hair in disarray, shirt collar open and tie blowing in the wind. 'I have approached those honourable men, the councillors, one of whom at least you would have thought would be concerned with your dilemma, and I stated your case, My Case.' He shouted above the crowd, who had become incensed when Philip told them that the members of the Council Chamber had told him not to be ridiculous, and that he should reserve his energy for his patients in his surgery. 'Me! Not to be ridiculous!' His arms now joined his tie and hair waving at the crowd, his sincere deep concern for the welfare of his patients and the community at large and his anger were written over his face How, he thought, would they cope if, left to their own devices, and what would then become of them? Philip at least put action after his thoughts and became spokesman for those who could not speak for themselves.

Listening to Philip speak, as well as to those who spoke before and after him, was one Jeremy Scott, a shrunken bald man, who because his spectacles were made up of thick lenses, was known to some as 'Pebbles'. His main function in life was to pry and spy, to snoop and report back to the members of the Trebovoir Green Council. Unmarried, unloved and unwanted, Mr Scott had a miserable disposition. As soon as he had digested all that was of interest to the Council committee, he trotted to reveal his new knowledge to the Mayor and his hangers-on, the sound of jeering and cat calls following his departure.

It was 5 pm and darkness had begun to close in on this damp and windy November day, when Jeremy Scott arrived at the private residence of the Mayor. whose name was Gladstone Stuart and who lived at 22 Leopold Grove, Woodford, a palatial house on the borders of London and Essex, but who also had an apartment attached to the Town Hall, paid for by the public. Jeremy Scott rang the bell of 22 Leopold Grove, the door opened and a pair of arms stretched out and yanked him inside. A coal fire was burning in the lounge, and, shivering Jeremy in his thin stained raincoat weather edged himself towards the comforting glowing flames. A wooden kitchen stool was produced for him to sit, Genoese velvet armchairs, the pride of the Mayor's furniture, were not for Jeremy's comfort. The Mayor's wife Lorna, gave Jeremy a cup of tea, not in one of her prized china cups, but in a tin mug. As Jeremy sipped the hot drink, the Mayor,

Gladstone Stuart, (formerly Stewart, but changed to make it look more aristocratic if spelt in the Royal manner) deftly put two one-pound notes into Jeremy's pocket.

Several members of the council's committee were guests of the Mayor and his wife that evening, and with Jeremy perched on the stool in their midst they proceeded to question, or rather to interrogate him as to the result of the Tower Hill gathering. Voices rose drowning Jeremy's answers, Gladstone shouting, "Gentlemen, please. Finally, the room quietened down. Pouring himself a glass of whisky from his peach-mirrored drinks cabinet, Gladstone, slowly turned and spoke to Jeremy. 'What...' said Gladstone, 'did the rabble leaders of the march have to say about the Old Peoples Home and of us?' Necks craned forwards, faces inches away from Jeremy's nose, as he in a fractured voice began to relate the days happenings and proceedings on Tower Hill. Voices were raised again when they realised that they were not the choice of the day in the eyes of the citizens of Trebovoir Green, nor were they at ease with the feelings of the people about their position as Coouncillors. The Mayor absorbed Jeremy's narrative of the day's events with deep concentrated thoughts, as minutes ticked by, he stroked his handlebar moustache, one arm across his chest and wandered about the room. He then took a deep breath, strode into the middle of the room and, like a grand Shakespearean actor, raised his arms for attention, and watched the expressions on the faces of the occupants of his large lounge as they turned from Jeremy to himself.

'Lorna,' he said to his wife, 'pour out drinks for our guests, I think that they might need one, while I see Jeremy out.' The door closing behind Jeremy again brought silence to the room. With their wives, the Mayor was entertaining thirty people, councillors, and those that benefitted by their association with the councillors. 'Gentlemen,' he addressed himself to the members of the council who were all men and not to their wives, he continued. 'When the young and the old unite they become very strong, rather than lose votes we must join them.'

'Traitor! Traitor!' a voice yelled. The wives, who were playing cards, brought their game of Whist to a halt. With an ear on the meeting heir eyes on the cards, they too joined the anti-march voice.

'Please,' shouted Gladstone. 'Please listen to me, and you will find out how it will work to our advantage.' Quietness descended around him, the drinks and the cards lowered in worried hands. Rain struck the window like pebble stones but not heavy enough to cause damage. He spoke, the sudden silence taking him by surprise, and making his first words break in their flow. 'Am I not a man of honour, have I not given my all to our advantage?' He waited, no sound came, only the nodding of anxious heads, he continued. 'Did I not persuade the people to elect you to remunerative offices on the council?' Again the silent nodding heads, like pigeons pecking for crumbs. 'My dear colleagues, what shall we do? Better stil, l I will tell what we shall do, we will demolish the old workhouse, ahem…' He cleared his throat, I mean 'Old Peoples Home, and rebuild it.'

'How, you may ask? In the first place we offer out tenders for the job.' His rhetorical questions puzzled his listeners, they were more attuned to bullying tactics than by sensible, rational discussion. Gladstone proceeded to enlighten them with his newly made plans, not only to appease the citizens of Trebovoir Green but also to make money. The next day in a closed secure room in the council offices he set out his programme. Councillors who had been his guests the night before were seated behind desks like school children. Also in the room were others who were not on any of the public committees, but were essential to the greater scheme, the money makers, builders, engineers, accountants, architects, and solicitors, all necessary for the projected plan which Gladstone was about to introduce to them.

'We,' said a more confidant Gladstone, 'will have to put in our own tender for the knocking down and for the re-building of the Home. It will also be our task to accept or reject designs and tenders, but whatever the case, we will only accept our own, which is in the capable hands of our own private company.' All present in the room smiled at the thought of their own consortium, devised and orchestrated by the Mayor only the previous year and yet to be employed on a scale big enough to make them money. After pointing out to them the scale of the project, and the benefits to them all, by drawing the details on a blackboard with white chalk, he finally turned around and asked them if they still wanted to go ahead with the plan.

'Yes! Yes!' they cried in unison. The news of the Town Hall's decision to build a new Home for the elderly spread like wildfire.

The following weeks were spent in negotiations and arguments; tenders for the work and designs for the building were delivered by numerous companies. A very convincing work party of scrutineers checked prices and designs, estimated times of completion and materials to be used, until the construction company of Lubar and Clarke, the private company of the councillors, was finally accepted.

Chapter Four

Mrs Greenbaum, Malka, lived not with her daughter, but opposite in a maisonette, a dwelling house built in the early 1920's for the workers, and divided into two flats with its own entrance. Malka's flat was different from the majority of the two up two down terraced houses; her maisonette was one of six in one block, with a road on either side of the block. One bedroom, a little room serving as parlour and kitchen in which there was a cast iron oven with a built-in fire to heat the saucepan and boil a kettle on the top hob. In the adjacent scullery there was a yellowish-brown butler sink, once used not only for washing up, but also as a bath for her children when they were babies. Looking round Malka's parlour one would immediately be confronted with the gleam from the cast iron oven, polished with black lead which made it shine like silver. A brass bedstead, with gargoyles on each corner, filled the bedroom which was separated from the parlour by a heavy dark curtain. Malka kept everything in her tiny flat spotlessly clean.

Nobody escaped her hospitality on visiting her modest home. As they entered her parlour a cup of tea was thrust into their hands, a homemade biscuit was proffered from a red and gold Victorian octagonal biscuit tin with a hinged lid. Silver sweet paper embellished frames on the photographs of her family Old, treasured birthday cards were also framed, adding to her individual decor, but only if the card had a pretty picture on it. At sixty-nine Malka was already looking older than her years, a widow for twenty-three years, yet she climbed up onto her dining table to stick back up the ceiling paper with sticky tape when it was falling down, great effort on her part.

She existed on her meagre pension and a weekly insult of five shillings from her son Morris, who stopped it when he realised that he would have to contribute to his mother's funeral. Her other children's help was very disappointing too, and invariably conspicuous by its absence when they 'forgot'. The clothes that she wore, were old fashioned, old, and repaired time and again with her skilful hands. If Malka would have utilised her nimble fingers for dressmaking, she might not have been subjected to such poverty. But such was her way of life, looking after her children, dusting, polishing, and making biscuits called, 'kichles', and cooking meals, was all that occupied her life. She made no demands on anyone but conducted her life in a quiet modest manner, oblivious of the world about her.

It was prior to her visit to the doctor that her children launched their major offensive against their mother, Malka Greenbaum. Gertie, her daughter, lived opposite and seldom called upon her own mother. The close set eyes of Gertie made her resemble a ravenous eagle, her mother Malka, her prey. 'Mother, you'll make life easier for all of us if you would go into that nice Home. We could visit you every week and bring you fruit and biscuits.' She looked at her two brothers, Sid and Morris, and nodded her head at them, a signal for them to voice their united front against their mother.

'Gertie's right, Mum,' they said in unison, and looked about the room but not daring to look at Malka, who, like a simmering volcano, began to explode. Malka started to shout, her hand holding her left breast as her palpitating heart began to react to this concerted move by her children to get her to leave her home and live in the disputed Old Peoples Home.

'Don't go on. don't say Ennytink Enny more. Ven did you evah visit me to see if I vos alife, Huhh!' Malka diminutive as she was, a Lilliputian in the land of giants, raised her voice to the heights of a gathering storm. She stood with her eyes focused on Gertie's neck, fingers poking at her daughter's body, a thin delicate, honest finger, pecking away, like a woodpecker at a telegraph pole. 'As for a nice home, pr'aps you vood like to try it out for six months, and if you like it, you might find it better than your own home and stay there for goot, eh! Neh!' Malka was shouting and pinching the tops of Gertie's arms, which was a habit every time that she lost her temper with her daughter.

'You'll regret this, Mother,' said Gertie, her face contorted with rage, and red patches of anger blossoming out over her cheeks, the inherited anger, a family trait, her voice screaming back to her mother as she descended the stairs, 'I'll have you committed to the home on doctor's orders, just you wait and see.' The door slammed behind her, her eyes wild with anger as she, in her pink fluffy slippers, slip slopping under her over-indulged frame entered into her own home, not too many yards away. Sidney and Morris, having tried to separate the two snarling women, also came under attack from Malka. She squared up to them, 'My dear children, luff for me you do not haff. I'm an embarrassment to you all, mine grandchildren don't come to see deir buba, dey don't know if

I I'm m alife, or dead. Old fashioned I may be, but at least I heff sometink vich none of you heff. I heff a soul. Now get aaht of mine 'ouse. Get Aaht.' Sid and Morris ignored Malka's demands and made a similar demand for her to go into the Home. She looked up to her son Sidney. 'Who are you? Ven did I last see you? Four years ago, was the first time in four years, so twice in eight years. Vott happened? Am I such a rich person dat now you vant to show me covert? (respect).'

She turned slowly, ever so slowly, a tigress approaching its prey. Morris, his jacket sitting tight about his body, hair from his belly popping itself through his non-iron nylon shirt which needed pressing, buttons hanging on desperately by the straining cotton thread. She looked at him with pitch black, eyes. 'You,' she snarled, 'my philanthropic son, if God should giff you back vot you gave to other people, you vould haff nuttink! Nuttink!' Malka's heart was pounding away, palpitating, racing as her sons closed the street door. Morris had allowed his mother five shillings a week until he was told that he would have to contribute to the funeral when she died, so he stopped it. The two sons followed their sister's slip-slopping pink slippers to her house across the street.

Malka, confused, worried and angry, unable to adjust to the thought of leaving her home went to the only place where she knew that she could receive solace, Dr Rabin's surgery, a sanctuary for the elderly, a brief escape from the traumas of family and officialdom.

Chapter Five

Cold wet weather greeted the demolition squad as it manoeuvred its way through the narrow streets to the Old People's Home. The last few men of the work team were heralded by the sound of cheers from the local citizens as the machinery to demolish the building was unloaded. As weeks passed, the solid Victorian structure gradually lessened in size. A large swinging iron ball suspended from a crane repeatedly swung back and forth hitting the walls with a deep, resonate crunch, accompanied by shouts of, 'Thar she goes!' The daily audience of the locals, covered in dust, regularly watched the workmen and cheered at every brick that was knocked down from the building. The ground surrounding the building was at the same time being levelled by bulldozers, until there was nothing left of the original structure. The debris then taken away left a blanket of brick dust and the site was fenced off ready for the next stage of work. A cloud of depression descended over the whole area, nobody spoke, or ventured to speak about the prospective new building which would, hopefully be built, but when? The subject was dropped like a red-hot lump of coal, as the old building disappeared and there was nothing more to be said or be complained about.

The people were victorious in having it pulled down, but was it to be a hollow victory?

January and February went by, but it was not until March that a revival of the rebuilding took place. Trucks with pilings, drills, cement mixers, bricks and all attendant paraphernalia began to arrive to the joy of the residents of Trebovoir Green. The sound of the machinery was music to those that would benefit from the rebuilt home, the senior citizens and their children looked upon the new building as a relief from the overcrowded houses which they shared and from then on, the responsibility of their parents' welfare would be in the hands of the local authority.

Malka was stirred with curiosity by the noise coming from the cleared site so she decided to investigate, and walked through the muddy streets, over disjointed paving stones and cobbled roads. It wasn't long before she stood in front of what was left of the old building. She watched, she looked, but her eyes saw only a grey dust covering the trees, a few trees, and some machinery. Malka, her eyes moist, felt her life slipping away. She was tired and disturbed by the treatment afforded her by her children. As she lifted her head up, she focused on the cranes, the workmen and the dus, and there appeared, as if in a dream, a vision of the new Home, and, like Moses, she knew that it would be there, but that she, Malka, would not live to see it completed. Turning her back went home, drinking in the early spring sunlight, the people, the houses, even the petrified trees black against a background of grey dust. She felt she had lived too long, she was now contented to go home and die. The sights seen for the last time were never to be seen again.

Two days went by, and Malka's neighbour, Ms Sophia Cooper, became very worried when the daily putting out of empty milk bottles from Malka's flat, an everyday chore, carried on as a way of life for every household, was not happening Neither had she heard any sound coming from Malka's flat although Malka liked her music and Sophia could often hear her singing along to the radio. Nor, for that matter, had she seen any sign of Malka at all. Sophie ran across the road to Gertie, Malka's daughter, and knocked loudly on the door. I'm coming! I'm coming!' shouted Gertie, wondering what all the fuss was about. The neighbours who were not used to door knockers being used so loudly, unless in an emergency, and this sounded like an emergency, started to appear at windows and in their doorways. The women poured out of their homes when they saw Gertie and Sophie Cooper run across the road to Malka's flat. Gertie, aware of the importance of the occasion, and of herself being the centre of attention, acted the full part of a distressed loving daughter, and the women folk kept at a respectful distance as they made their way to Malka's front door. Hand on breast, feet encased in her pink slippers, tears travelling down her cheeks, and stockings loose about her legs, even at this moment she was reluctant to move up the stairs to her mother's flat. 'Come on Luv,' said Sophie, gently pushing Gertie, up the dimly lit staircase. Bhind, in order of acquaintance, the other women followed. Slowly, ever so slowly, the women followed Gertie and Sophia into the parlour Pushing the heavy curtain aside they entered Malka's bedroom and the noise of the women climbing the stairs suddenly stopped. Silence descended upon them as they looked at the toothless, grey and shrivelled face of Malka, an old woman lying on her bed, the brass rails at the head and the foot surmounted by large brass knobs shining and reflecting the distorted faces on their surface. 'Mummy! Mummy!' cried Gertie, now truly disturbed at the sight of her dying mother. There was no dry eye visible in Malka's bedroom as Gertie and Sophie tidied the bed, rasping sounds escaping from her mother's mouth. Hers were visible on her chin, which was always plucked clean of them when she was active. Tea, the cure for all English ills, the solace for all English souls, was being made in the tiny scullery when the doctor arrived. He pronounced her dead.

Gareth

Prologue, 1944

The cold wind blew over the gravel compound accompanied by a damp drizzle of rain as Sturmbannführer Karl Bauer, who was an officer in the German Army, an equivalent rank to that of a Major in the British army, boots crunching on gravel, walked across the compound. Major Bauer, was being held a Prisoner of War in a camp in the north of England. The prison camp was enclosed with barbed wire fences and patrolled by armed guards, strangely at odds with the surrounding quintessential English countryside. The German prisoners could only look out upon open land, distant woodlands and farms. The silence of the land was often broken when aircraft took to the air from airfields across the country to carry out bombing raids over Germany.

His hands clasped behind his back; Major Bauer walked nonchalantly towards a new arrival of German prisoners who were being offloaded from several army trucks. Bauer had been a prisoner of war for two years and was the most senior German officer in the camp at that time. He was therefore accepted, by virtue of his rank, as the liaison and negotiating officer between the British military and the German prisoners.

As a German high-ranking officer, and a gentleman of upper class, he maintained he was entitled to a batman-valet to tend his every need. He made similar demands for privileges to be extended to the other German officers, private dining facilities, separate sleeping quarters, toilets, bathrooms, and radios. Consequently, Bauer was often summoned to the camp Commander's office to discuss his seemingly unacceptable requests. He was looked upon by his captors as an eccentric German officer and was frequently reprimanded by the commander of the camp for what were considered his outrageous demands. Or was there an ulterior motive, a hidden agenda, behind his eccentric behaviour?

Bauer, and several other German officers, introduced themselves to this new arrival of prisoners, and divided them into small groups. Bauer and his officers then walked quite casually with them to their designated billets where they were to be held. Speaking to them unusually quietly and with their heads lowered, the German officers explained to the newcomers the reason for their strange behaviour, which was the fact that there were hidden microphones in the camp, in the sleeping huts, in the dining huts, in the latrines and showers, and scattered around the compound.

Among these new prisoners was one who particularly interested Bauer. This new prisoner held a Nazi Rank of Waffen-SS-Sturmbannführer, equivalent to that of a Company sergeant major. Bauer also noticed that the thumb on this sergeant major's' right hand, and half of his right ear, had been cut off, leaving a ragged scar which ran down his cheek to the corner of his mouth.

Chapter One
1916

There was an agreed two-hour truce, and the guns fell silent across the battlefield allowing both the British and the German soldiers to collect their wounded. The open land between them was pockmarked with bomb craters into which many of the wounded had taken refuge, some of whom were too far away and too close to the German trenches to be rescued. The cries of the wounded wanting to be saved echoed across the now silent war zone, but a two-hour truce might not save lives if you were too far away to be spotted and returned to the safety of your own lines. It was likened to a death sentence. Gareth Alun Jones of the Welsh County Regiment of Volunteers lay in one of these bomb craters beneath the bodies of two of his dead comrades, his former boyhood friends. Gareth, wounded in both legs, was too weak to crawl out of the bomb crater or even to shout out loud for help.

Then he heard voices above, but they were speaking German not English. He was afraid that if they found him, they would kill him, he did not know what to do. Young, cold, wet, wounded and weak, he began to cry. The thought of being shot was frightening, a that thought kept spinning around in his head. His sobs were heard by German soldiers, who, like the British, were searching for their own wounded. He screamed out in pain as he felt the German soldiers, not realising his legs were injured and trapped beneath the dead men, grasp his arms and pull him out of the crater.

Stretched out on the edge of the crater, Gareth found himself surrounded by German soldiers looking down at him as if he were a curious specimen. Gareth resigned himself to being shot. With his eyes closed and tears running down his cheeks, he started quietly to say the Lord's Prayer, 'Ein Tad, yr hwn yn y nefoedd.' He prayed in Welsh, as he had done every day as a child. Then he heard a voice joining him in prayer, the last words of that prayer. 'YN oesoedd, Amen.'

'Forever, Amen.' This also in Welsh. Opening his eyes, he looked up into the face of a smiling German officer. 'You are now a prisoner of war, and for you the war is over,' said the officer. Gareth was placed on a stretcher and carried to a field hospital behind the German lines away from the shells, bullets and bombs. The condition of the field hospital was primitive, with moaning and crying patients laid out in rows on a wet field alongside the dead and the dying. But for Gareth, this was salvation, the answer to his prayers.

He had been lying on the stretcher sleeping and waking in what seemed to him as a horrific dream, when a familiar voice asked for his name and his age. Looking round he saw the German officer who spoke Welsh, and who introduced himself to Gareth as Hauptmann Albert Bauer, the equivalent rank to that of a British Captain. He asked the wounded soldier his name and his age. Gareth turning his head away said 'Gareth,' and unconvincingly, 'seventeen.' The Captain knelt on the wet grass beside the boy soldier on the stretcher, placed his arm around his shoulder and said softly, 'What is your true age?' The boy, not yet a man lying in front of him had looked away when first asked his age, he now hesitated and whispered, 'Fifteen.' and began to cry. The comforting arm of Captain Bauer around Gareth's shoulders was akin to that of a Father and son. Captain Bauer enlightened Gareth with his command of the Welsh and English language when he said, 'I lived in Cardiff in Wales for four years, with my mother and father when my father was teaching German language students the history of architecture in Germany. I also attended school in Cardiff from 1898 and became conversant with the English and Welsh languages.'

Gareth was eventually transferred to a hospital where he underwent surgery to repair his wounds, after which he was transferred to a Prisoner of War Camp. Whilst he was in the hospital Captain Bauer had visited him and was saddened by the story of this young man's upbringing and how he and his friends thought that being a soldier would be a great change from the orphanage, exciting and fun.

Gareth had been sent to an orphanage at the age of six, with no knowledge of his parents, or of any other relatives. The orphanage resembled that of a Victorian Workhouse. Children were given a basic education until they reached the age of ten when they were marched to factories and the coal mines, the money for their labour was sent to the orphanage. At the end of their work shift they were marched back to the orphanage, where they had their meagre meals. The staff at this orphanage lacked compassion and friendship. The daily regime was laced with shouts, slaps across the face, hands held out to be caned and sexual abuse. Gareth and two friends escaped from the orphanage, by removing the iron window grill and climbing out of the window to freedom aged thirteen.

They worked on the farms and down the mines, in the winter they slept on bales of hay in barns, and outhouses, in the summer, they slept in the fields amongst the haystacks. When war was declared in 1914 the three boys tried to enlist into the army but were too young. It was in October 1916 that they were able to finally enlist giving their ages as seventeen. The recruiting sergeants were desperately aware of the need to replace the many thousands of soldiers killed and wounded in battle; they therefore closed their eyes to the age of the volunteers. If they could stand, march, and hold a gun they were accepted, and for these three boys they were now in the army, the Welsh County Regiment of Volunteers. The three boys now had clothes, food and a bed to sleep in. This luxury did not last very long, as the demand for reserves to replace the many soldiers killed on the front line was becoming an urgency which demanded constant replenishing. Gareth and his friends were shipped across the channel with thousands of soldiers from regiments formed in villages, cities, colleges, universities, indeed from all over the country.

Chapter Two

Gunfire could be heard growing louder as the troop ship that they were on approached nearer the French coast.

Disembarking from the troopships the soldiers formed up in their regiments and marched to their designated battle zones. As they marched to the fields of conflict, they passed wounded soldiers who were marching out. A contradiction in terms, not marching, but struggling to move in lines of bandaged, blinded and on stretchers. Gareth and his friends began to feel the pangs of fear as the trenches came into view where bodies mutilated by shells and bombs were draped over the edge of those trenches.

The next day, after a sleepless night in the trenches, the order came to advance, with a warning, that if they returned without their rifles they would be shot for cowardice. The three friends were pushed forward by the pressure of riflemen behind them and found themselves way ahead of their regiment and ended up in a bomb crater under heavy machine gun fire. Shaking with fear, unable to steady their guns, they became targets for the German artillery. Gareth was shot in the legs and his two friends fell on top of him, both killed. Such was the story that Gareth told to Captain Bauer when he visited him in hospital.

The Captain asked Gareth where he lived in England, or for that matter in Wales. The answer that he received shocked him, for Gareth said, 'I have no home in England or in Wales, I lived in an orphanage until I ran away and lived with my friends in barns on farms, and outhouses in fields until we went into the Army.'

Sitting beside Gareth's bed, the Captain bent forward, his head in his hands, unable to comprehend the life of this child soldier, now lying wounded in a hospital bed beside him.

'I must arrange for you to stay in this hospital and not be transferred to a prisoner of war camp,' said the Captain. 'And I will visit you again.' He then stood up and left.

The Captain did not return, and Gareth was sent to a POW camp. Life inside the camp was primitive but better than Gareth had expected, he had a bed, regular food and the company of sympathetic brother soldiers, they referred to him, because of his young age and height, as Kitten.

Chapter Three

It was on Friday the 15th of November 1918, the weather cold with threatening showers, when orders were given by the senior British officers in the camp to pack up possessions and march out of the Zossen Prisoner of War Camp to freedom. News of the German surrender four days earlier had only just arrived by allied dispatch riders. The German guards had quickly left the camp during the night after receiving the same, but delayed, news of the German surrender. The Zossen camp had held captive a mixture of 1,500 prisoners, British, American and French soldiers. The war had ended, hostilities had ceased, and the guns had fallen silent four days earlier, on the eleventh day of the eleventh month at the eleventh hour. British and American soldiers were now being taken to Calais and Dunkirk where they would board ships for Dover and England.

The liberated soldiers marched out of the camp through the streets of Zossen, where the local people stood in silence. Through this silent crowd came a man who pushed himself forward, his sharp eyes searching the marching soldiers until they fell on Gareth, when he rushed forward, thrust a package into Gareth's hands then ran away.

The next day, the morning of Saturday 16th of November, after a wet weather channel crossing, the soldiers disembarked from the crowded wet decks of the ships in the harbour of Dover. They were greeted by a military band fanfare, cheers and tears from waiting families, friends, and bystanders. They were home, after their years spent in a German prisoner of war camp.

The disembarking soldiers were given tea and biscuits, after which they were directed to areas where their regiments were rallying. Dover quay was a scene of confusion as soldiers and families tried to meet and then locate their regiments. There was no great rush, and compassion was shown to these one-time prisoners of war. Eventually, late in the day, the soldiers, most of whom had located their regiments, were marched to their trains and transported back to their barracks, which were dotted around the country.

Gareth, like many returning soldiers, had no one to meet him He drank his tea, ate his biscuits and located the rallying point of the Welsh County Regiment of Volunteers, then boarded the train for Wales.

Back at camp the returning soldiers were welcomed by a guard of honour, comprising camp Commanding Officer, officers, non-commissioned officers, and soldiers of the regiment. The soldiers Mess that day was noisy with men greeting, consoling each other, and drinking to their repatriation.

Gareth found a quiet corner in his barrack hut; whilst the rest of the occupants were away drinking in the canteen bar. The silence was palpable now he was back in camp, no gunfire, the war was over. Just the sound of the rain slapping against the windows, the droplets of which catching the last of the evening light as they slid down the glass windowpanes like crystals. Gareth unpacked his kitbag, removed the strange package that was thrust into his hands as he left the Zossen Prison camp and placed it on the table. He was still unaware of the identity of the man who had thrust the package into his hands as he marched out of the POW camp. Untying the string that held the package together, he tentatively removed an envelope from the package, it had his name on it, Gareth Alun Jones. He had never, ever, received a letter, or had any other form of correspondence from anybody in his life before or since escaping from the orphanage. He had lived the life of a hermit until he went into the army. The army was his life, food, clothes, bed, comradeship discipline and respect. He slowly ran his fingers over his name on the envelope. With his hands shaking, he removed the letter from the envelope, it was a precious moment. Gareth was taught to read and write under a harsh regime in his years spent in the orphanage. His lessons were primarily reading and writing, all under the threat of being slapped around the head if he spelt a word wrong or spoke out of turn. The letter was from Captain Albert Bauer, and it began with an apology from the Captain as to why he did not visit Gareth in the hospital. 'Dear Gareth, I did return to the hospital, but it was empty of all the patients and closed. Patients and nursing staff had been evacuated away from the fighting. I did not know to which prison camp you were sent. By then my wife had died from the disease called Spanish Flu, which had killed more people around the world than the 1914–1918 war. I did, however, locate the prisoner of War Camp where you were sent, through several POW detention lists, which were filed in the offices of the Central Berlin Prisoner of War camps. I live just a few miles away and knew the officer in charge who let me peruse the lists, and eventually, I finally located you and your camp.'

The Captain first enquired after Gareth's health and then explained why he wanted to keep in touch with him. It transpires that the Captain had family in England also named Bauer. The Bauer family had fled Russia during the murdering Pogroms in the early 19th century; some went to Germany and some to England. Gareth had to look up the meaning of the word Pogrom in a dictionary as he had never heard of it before, he read that it referred to the massacre of Jews in Russia and Eastern Europe. The Captain's letter continued with an invitation for Gareth to contact the Bauer family in England. The Captain had explained to the Bauer family who lived in London, that this young boy had no family or a home to go to. He had fought for his country and had been wounded, and he asked if they would be prepared to contact him and invite him the stay with them for a few days.

Gareth was puzzled how the Captain was able to communicate with his Bauer family in England when the end of the war was just a few weeks back. The Captain must have anticipated Gareth's question of communication between the two countries at war with each other, because he explained that some friends of the family who had also fled the Pogroms had settled in Switzerland. Switzerland being neutral, postal communication was possible between the families, and had continued during the war through friendly family connections via the Swiss, postal offices. As he read the letter his mind went back to the years he had spent in the orphanage, and this was the first time that someone had shown compassion for him, and that person was a German, a German officer, an enemy during the war, who stopped his men from shooting him, and who had saved his life and who now, after the war, still had his welfare at heart. Gareth had difficulty in comprehending the motive of this person, why me, what have I done to deserve this attention? He read on, as Captain Bauer explained in the letter, that he and his wife had no children, and after his wife died, he had no family in Germany, as most of the Bauer family that came from Russia had stayed for just a short time in Germany, and then went and resettled in America. Albert Bauer having married, his wife being German, remained in Germany with his wife. Being Jewish, there was always a reluctance to fraternise with his wife's non-Jewish relatives, who appeared to ostracise his wife when they got married. This was the first time that Gareth new of his saviour's religion, having never before met a Jew or even knew how a Jew looked. He continued to read the letter. 'My family in England have a son and a daughter, both at university, so they too are lonely, and they are the only Bauer's in London. When I wrote relating your life or lack of life to them, they asked me if I could contact you and invite you to spend a day or two with them. If I have offended you by telling them of your early life with no family, I apologise. However, should you wish to take advantage of their hospitality I have enclosed an envelope with their address written on it. I look forward to hearing from you. Kindness, Albert Bauer.'

Gareth placed everything that he had taken out of his Kitbag back into it, even the letter from the Captain, not wishing, just yet, to answer the letter or writing to the Captain's family in London, until he had settled back at camp and recovered from the aftereffects of being wounded and his friends killed.

It was three weeks into the new year, January 1919, when Gareth was informed by his sergeant, that he must attend the station headquarters. On arrival he was summoned into the CO's office. To say that Gareth was apprehensive would have been an understatement. Questions upon questions were buzzing around in his head. What had he done wrong, what had he forgotten? Was there anything that he was supposed to do and had forgotten to do. And why was the sergeant smiling?

Marching with the sergeant into the office, ordered by the sergeant to stand to attention, then told to salute the CO, Captain Radcliff. Gareth began to feel queasy. He then looked up when the Captain said, 'Stand easy soldier.' He too was smiling, as were the other officers in the room.

'Private Gareth Alun Jones,' said Captain Radcliff, 'you are now promoted to Lance Corporal of the Welsh County Regiment of Volunteers, and I have much pleasure in presenting you with your stripes.'

Gareth had been employed in the adjutant's office since returning from Germany, writing up a report of the battle in which he was involved and wounded, and in that precise report, listed the casualties and the number of soldiers taken prisoner during that campaign. He had attracted the attention of his senior officers who were impressed by the way Gareth, with a photographic memory, was able to record the events during that campaign to which he was witness, and also the incompetence of the commanders in the field, for ordering the soldiers to march, in what amounted to, a wall of machine gun fire. The report was so professionally written that the officers quite rightly thought that this young man had a good future in the and would progress to a higher position quickly. Also. his command of the English language, spelling, grammar and copperplate handwriting so impressed the headquarters staff to the extent that he was recommended for promotion. His few short years spent in the orphanage under a strict regime of reading, writing, and an emphasis on English grammar, certainly manifested itself at a later age, and become recognised for promotion to that of Lance Corporal at a young age of 18 years.

It was after receiving his stripe that Gareth told the CO, about Captain Bauer, and how he had saved his life. Captain Radcliff looked up, nodded to his second in command and asked Gareth to make a full report relating to this German officer, and hand that finished report to the station headquarters as soon as it was completed.

After settling down in his own Corporal's room, Gareth eventually got around to reading the letter from the Captain. The Corporal's room, which Gareth was now in, was in fact an extension of the main barrack hut. It had a table, chair, locker cupboard and a bed. Gareth looked around the room he now occupied in disbelief, his own private room. The first time that he had had the privacy of his own bedroom. Gareth read the letter from Captain Bauer once more, but this time with a clear mind. He decided to answer the letter and to contact the Captain's family in London.

He was due for a week's leave and thought that it would be nice to spend a few days in London, a city that he had heard so much about but had never had the opportunity to visit. The bonus was that he, being a serving soldier had a travel warrant which allowed him to travel free on the trains, and because of the German Captain, accommodation with his Bauer family.

Gareth received a letter from the London Bauer family, which he collected from the camp station post office, just ten days after he had written to them. They acknowledged his letter and invited him to stay with them for a few days. So it was on February the Sixth 1919, a very cold and wet Thursday, that Gareth, who had accepted their invitation to stay with the Bauer family, arrived at Paddington Station As he walked down the platform towards the exit, he saw a man waving a large white signboard with the name 'Gareth' in large print on it. Beneath that signboard was Leonard Bauer who, seeing Gareth in his army uniform waving back, vigorously waved the signboard even more so, and smiled.

The taxi ride from Paddington station to the Bauer's house in Maida Vale took only 20 minutes. As the taxi pulled up outside the house, number 14 Blomfield Place, the door was thrown open and Mrs Zina Bauer ran out to meet them with a smiling face and an umbrella to protect them from the rain.

Chapter Four

On returning to his barracks in Wales, Gareth sat back on his chair in the Corporal's room and reminisced over the few enjoyable days that he had spent in London with the Bauer family: Gareth marvelled at the sites that he was taken to, such as the Houses of Parliament, Buckingham Palace, Westminster Abbey, and the Tower of London, just some of the many historic sites he saw, and was amazed at the vast number of people in London jostling each other in the streets. He had bought Zina, Mrs. Bauer, a bunch of flowers from a florist in a nearby street, as a token of gratitude for inviting him to stay the weekend with them and he really hoped to see them again soon.

On the Monday following his return to camp, Gareth was told to report to the CO's office. On entering the office, he addressed his commanding officer with usual military formalities, and waited. 'Lance Corporal,' said Captain Radcliff, 'did you have a successful weekend in London?'

To which Gareth smiled, and said, 'I did, Sir. And it was more than I had ever expected.' Sitting in the office, in front of the Captain's desk was a man in civilian clothes.

Captain Radcliff invited Gareth to sit down, which he did, beside this other man, both of whom were waiting for the

Captain to speak. Radcliff introduced Gareth to the man as Lieutenant Michaels but had not informed him of the department or regiment to which Lieutenant Michaels was connected.

'I must enlighten you Lance Corporal Jones, that I have been corresponding with Captain Albert Bauer, not only in thanking him for protecting one of my soldiers, your good self, and offering you the hospitality of his family in Britain, but of the consequences taking place in Germany after the cease fire in November 1918.'

Lieutenant Michaels and Gareth, wore faces of puzzlement, not knowing what would come next, and when Captain Radcliff spoke again, they were shocked by his revelations of the new Germany. Captain Radcliff said, 'A Treaty will be signed between the Allies and Germany on June 28th, 1919. However, the devaluation of the German currency, strikes, mass unemployment, denuding of Germany's industrial machinery by the allies, shortage of food, the abdication of Kaiser Wilhelm on the ninth of November 1918 and the defeat of Germany on the eleventh, two days later, have led to the rise of the Weimar Republic. Captain Bauer told me in his letter,' continued Radcliff, 'that many Germans believed that socialists, liberals, academics, Jews, scientists etc, were the cause of Germany losing the war and mobs of criminals were rampaging around the streets beating up people who they thought were the cause of that defeat.' Radcliff came to the essence of the meeting when he said that Germany was secretly rearming, and that the British Intelligence mechanism was not at its best. 'Captain Bauer, being a Jew, and a German officer, albeit retired, still had access to military information which he is ready to impart to us through safe channels. This is where you, Lance Corporal Jones, come in. Lieutenant Michaels will be seconded to the new British Embassy in Berlin, and you in theory, will be one of the clerks working in the embassy, but you will be living with Captain Bauer as his relative.'

Gareth could not believe what he was hearing, after all, he could speak Welsh and English but certainly not German. To Gareth's relief he was not expected to go to Germany until the spring of 1920 after the Embassy had been restored. It had been set on fire during the 1919 political riots as were many government buildings and embassies. What the Captain did explain to both men sitting in front of him, was, that they would now attend German language speaking lessons. Gareth was also informed that he would be going to Germany early in the next year. Captain Radcliff said that he had arranged for him to stay with Albert Bauer and become proficient in the local dialect and not speak German with a Welsh accent. 'Lance Corporal Jones,' said the Captain, 'by the end of the year you will be promoted to sergeant, as befits the office that you will be attached to, the Military Intelligence department.' Gareth was astounded at his rapid elevation from Lance Corporal to sergeant, leap frogging that of Corporal Nevertheless, he could not help but feel apprehensive about going to Germany whilst there were riots and beatings in the streets.

Chapter Five
Berlin

In the spring of 1920 Captain Radcliff accompanied Gareth to Dover where he would embark on a ferry to Calais. On the way to Dover, the Captain, who was sitting beside Gareth in the chauffeur driven officer's car, said that he was impressed with the report he had received from the military school of languages, except for the fact that Gareth spoke German with a slight Welsh accent.

On arrival in Calais Gareth made his way through the crowded Custom Hall, wondering if he would recognise the Captain Bauer, who he had not seen since 1916, four years earlier. Then there was a tap on his shoulder which made him turn around quickly. The memory of seeing Captain Bauer briefly, on the battlefield and then in the hospital, did not for a moment register, until he saw that infectious smile of the Captain, which Gareth first saw when he heard a voice accompanying him in his Welsh prayer in 1916 on the battlefield. Prematurely grey at twenty-four, the Captain shook Gareth's hand and remarked that he was impressed that in four years the boy soldier had grown into tall, smart looking man. The greeting was mixed with laughter as Gareth returned the compliments in German, but with a Welsh accent, to which the Captain, who spoke Welsh, replied in Welsh with a German accent. Captain Bauer told Gareth to call him Albert and that his stay in Berlin would improve his German. On the train to Berlin from Calais, Albert, as Gareth had been invited to call him, had booked them into a private dining carriage on the train, and as they dined Gareth was given details of his duties related to the intelligence department in London. He had also been given a German passport and name, the documents of which he was to collect from the British Embassy in Berlin. Gareth asked Albert what name did he have? With a sly grin, Albert said, 'You are my cousin, Karl Bauer, from Hamburg.' Albert Bauer had followed in his father's footsteps; and he too, was now a lecturer in classic German architecture. Gareth was told that he would be introduced into the subtleties of that classic historic profession, should anyone care to ask, out of curiosity, what he was doing in Berlin. With Albert polishing his German and giving him books to read in German about architecture, he would be able to blend in with the German society.

Chapter Six

Every three months Gareth returned to London with his reports of German plans to rearm, and the thuggish extremes of violence from the Nazi Brown Shirts, Hitler's private army, as well as the countrywide political unrest. All these were delivered by hand to the designated intelligence offices in Baker Street Place, Marylebone. Captain Radcliff said that he deemed it safer and more secure as he did not trust some of the staff in the British Embassy in Berlin. It was Lieutenant Michaels who raised the suspicion that there might be one or two German sympathisers within the embassy complex.

With his blonde hair and penetrating blue eyes, Gareth was able to pass as a true blooded German and attend Nazi meetings. His photographic memory came into the fore when writing his reports, recording the speakers and in many cases their supporters, all of whom wanted a pure German race, purity of blood, pure Aryan.

The rise of Aryan extremism was a threat to Communists, Liberals, Jews, gypsies, all opposition parties and many others who did not conform to this extreme Nazi doctrine. Gareth, in 1932, having attended one of these meetings, advised Albert to leave the counter. Albert said that he would give it some thought as he had noticed that many of his Jewish friends were packing their belongings and preparing to leave from the land t for which their families had fought and died. Captain Albert Bauer looked at the photographs on the mantel shelf of himself, proudly wearing his medals on his German officer's uniform in World War One. Tears formed in his eyes, he looked at Gareth and just said, 'What for?' – Pointing at his picture, and again saying – 'what for?'

On bright, warm Spring Monday afternoon in May 1933, Gareth, who had spent the weekend in the British embassy in Berlin with Lieutenant Michaels, had been busy writing out his report, and was then walking towards Albert's house, where he had been living, on and off since, 1920, when he heard shouting and screams. As he ran towards the noise, his briefcase bumping against his side, Gareth saw a fight taking place between four Brown Shirt thugs and a man now lying on the ground being kicked and punched. As he got closer, he heard the man pleading for the thugs to stop kicking him when one of them produced a knife and plunged it into the man's neck. Gareth recognised the victim as Albert. With great speed Gareth charged into the thugs and started to fight them off snatching the knife from one thug and using it to fight back. He slashed the face of the knife holder cutting half of his ear off, slicing his face from the ear to his mouth, and as the thug tried to protect his face with his right hand, Gareth slashed again, this time cutting the thumb off of the right hand. The four Brown Shirts ran away screaming, their bodies cut and covered with blood where Gareth had cut them.

Albert lay silent, dead at his feet, the curtains and shutters of the houses in the street drawn and closed, since nobody wanted to be a witness After all, Albert was just a Jew, and in 1933 Jews were the scapegoats for all Germany's ills. Gareth bent down and placed his arms around Albert's shoulders. He kissed his head and began to sing in Welsh a mournful prayer, loud enough to penetrate the drawn curtains and closed shutters. Later that day he planned for Albert to be buried with his wife. He stayed in the house for a few days gathering Albert's personal belongings and then reported to Lieutenant Michaels at the embassy. Gareth returned to England where he contacted the Bauer family, related to them the details of Albert's death, and gave them the suitcase containing Albert's personal belongings.

Because of his fluency in speaking German, by then with a German accent, Gareth was attached to the military intelligence Those who were attached to this section of the army were radio and telephone specialists, tapping into German military radio and telephone communications and sending misinformation back to Germany. When war was declared on the third of September 1939, Gareth found himself in charge of that intelligence department. He was sent to Africa in 1941 as an interrogator of German prisoners of war during the desert campaign. However, there was need for more information of a personal kind, and it was decided that Gareth should adopt the guise of a German officer in a new prisoner of war camp for German officers and senior non-commissioned officers in Lancashire, in the north of England.

And so, it was, that in 1942 Sturmbannführer Karl Bauer who was supposedly captured in Italy, became the senior German POW officer in that prison camp in Lancashire.

Chapter Seven

A rumour went around this Lancastrian prisoner of war camp that one of the prisoners was giving information about German military positions in France to the British. This suspicion came about when one of the prisoners picked up a piece of paper in the compound with lists of the German defences along the French coast. Major Karl Bauer ordered six of the senior German officers to meet him in his private room. The conclusion of this meeting was that it had to be one of the new arrivals of prisoners, but which one? It did not take too long to identify the culprit, as more pieces of paper were found in the latrines after one of the prisoners was leaving and had forgotten to flush the toilet. It was when the German prisoners were in the compound, that the six officers searched this suspect's bed and found more evidence of the German traitor.

Early next morning the major was woken by shouts coming from the wash and toilet hut. Quickly dressing he ran to where the shouts were coming from, pushing through the group of onlookers, he saw the culprit with his throat cut. He also noticed he had one half of an ear cut off, a knife scar down his face and the thumb on his right hand was cut off.

The major smiled to himself and walked away. The spreading of clues to the murderer of Captain Albert Bauer, by dropping pieces of paper in the known areas where this Brown Shirt Nazi frequented, was a success. As he walked away, he looked up into the sky and said, 'Rest in peace, Albert.'

A week later there was a commotion in the compound when four red capped military police, followed by ten armed soldiers, marched into the compound. Round the perimeter of the camp there were more armed soldiers. The prisoners were ordered to stand in line against the perimeter fence. They watched as the soldiers went into the huts, wondering what they were looking for.

They were shocked when soldiers emerged from Major Karl Bauer's hut with the major in handcuffs. Behind him came two soldiers carrying what looked like a wireless with lengths of wires or aerials, dangling from it. On a closer examination it could have been noticed that the radio was a theatrical prop made of cardboard. As they marched past the prisoners near the fence, an object fell to the ground from the wireless. No one moved to pick it up until the soldiers left. One officer who was closest, bent down and retrieved the object which was a Morse code key tapper. The key was deliberately dropped to enhance the guilt of Major Karl Bauer.

That evening, the commander of the POW camp summoned the senior German officers to his office. He informed them that the British intelligence had been tracking signals coming from around twenty square miles of the POW camp, and it was finally found to come from this camp. He went on to say that Major Karl Bauer had adapted the radio that was given to him, to transmit by Morse code information of the number British aircraft that flew over the camp leaving these shores to bomb Germany. He then said that the major would stand trial and if found guilty he would be executed.

Two weeks later, having been found guilty of spying, Major Karl Bauer was taken to a remote area away from the camp to be executed. The German prisoners of war had lined the compound and sang the German national anthem, many with tears in their eyes. The major had been like a Father confessor to them. He heard about their families and their regiments, and about the German defences along the French coast. The Firing squad had marched past the gates of the camp with the handcuffed Major minutes before, and later after the guns had fired, the German soldiers stood to attention as the truck carrying the Major's coffin drove slowly past the prison. With a shout the compound lined with the prisoners gave the German salute, not knowing that the coffin was empty.

Major Karl Bauer removed his German uniform in the Commander's house, situated a mile from the camp, and he then clothed himself in the uniform of Major Gareth Alun Jones of the Welsh County Regiment of Volunteers. After dinner with the commander, and a few days of well-earned rest, Gareth returned to London where he had arranged to meet Leonard and Zina Bauer at the Officer's Club in Piccadilly, where they were to be his guests for lunch. To their surprise, Gareth told them that they would be accompanying him to Buckingham Palace the following week where His Majesty, King George VI would be awarding him with the DSO, the "Distinguished Service Order" for meritorious conduct.

Not Me, Not I

Buy a poppy my friend, Not me not I,
I don't want to fight and die.
Buy a poppy my friend, wear with prominence,
And I'll tell of some soldiers that went to the continent.
They fought in rain they fought in mud,
the poppy is red the colour of blood.
Please don't say that it makes me cry,
I don't want to fight and die,
Not me, Not I

With a song and a wave, they went away, some came back
But many stayed.
Buy a poppy my friend, pin it on your vest,
If you lose a leg in battle, they stick a medal on your chest.
It makes you sick, it makes you sigh that young men,
old men, had to die,
I didn't want to fight
Not me, Not I

War to end all wars, they said,
Did they lose sons, did they count the dead?
Buy a poppy my friend, it grows in a field
where the dead are buried without, their shields.
I'm buried here, in the field where I died
Not far from the trench where I cried
I didn't want to die
Not me, Not I

The Silence of Gilda

War had been raging throughout Europe since the First of September 1939, when Germany invaded Poland in breach of an agreement which Hitler had made with Neville Chamberlain, then Prime Minister of Great Britain, on the 30th September 1938. The German armies quickly marched across Europe. Because of that breach of the agreement, Britain and France declared war on Germany on the third September 1939. The Southeast Asian theatre of war is said to have begun in July 1937 when Japan invaded China and conflict rose to a new level following the raid on Pearl Harbour and simultaneous attacks on Hong Kong, the Philippines, Thailand, Singapore and Malaya on the seventh and eight of December 1941.

Part One

Burma, December 1944

The Fourteenth Army in the Far East known by the sobriquet, 'the Forgotten army', were fighting to free Burma from the Japanese. It became known as the longest and deadliest continuous battle in World War Two. This "forgotten army", was comprised of soldiers from, Britain, India, and Africa.

The Allied armies were also fighting the Indian Nationalist Army, many of whom had been trained by the Japanese, and fought beside them against the Allies. Indians, who were Japanese prisoners of war, were persuaded to join the Japanese and fight the British to win back their independence. They all fought in the same harsh conditions in the dense jungle. Soldiers from both sides succumbed to the effects of the wet humid heat and weakened by limited food supplies and polluted drinking water, they suffered a multitude of ailments, malaria, dysentery, Dengue Fever snake bites, leeches and jungle foot rot.

Field hospitals in the Burmese jungle were a scattered collection of canvas tents divided into First Aid units. One first aid tent had a ward to accommodate ten patients, a treatment room and a basic operating theatre. Field hospitals were the first point of call for medical treatment in the jungle, a centre which prepared patients to be flown to hospitals in India and after receiving treatment, subject to their medical condition, returned to their regiments or embark on ships back to England.

On Christmas Day 1944, in one jungle medical unit there were six patients, two suffering from malaria and four recovering from combat wounds. The complement of medical staff was comprised of two medical doctors and six nurses, who were housed in adjoining smaller tents. The nurses and doctors had decided to cheer up the patients and the soldiers who were guarding this medical centre, by putting on a Christmas show. Linking arms, and led by one of the nurses called Gilda, the nurses formed a chorus line, and began dancing up and down the tent. As they sang and danced the patients laughed and clapped their hands. With her long blonde hair, pretty face, long legs showing her stockings and suspenders, just like a high kicking dancer on a London West End stage, Gilda stood out from the others. As she danced her hair flowed around her like a halo and some of those watching her said that she looked like a Hollywood film star.

Then Gilda announced, 'Let us all sing together, Underneath the Spreading Chestnut Tree.' Some of the patients managed to sit up in bed and join the doctors, nurses and the soldiers as they raised and stretched their arms above their heads in the action of wavering trees, keeping time with the words of the song. The laughter was hilarious.

And then, it suddenly stopped. Gunfire and screams were heard from outside the tent which instantly broke up the party, the side of the tent was ripped open and twelve Japanese soldiers burst in. They looked at the nurses in their fancy, scanty costumes, saw the bandaged wounded soldiers in the beds, and charged at the beds. The nurses screamed as the Japanese began shooting and bayoneting the helpless patients.

The patients tried to avoid the sharp blades, but they were cut to pieces, beds were soaked with blood, and their bodies dragged outside the tent and dumped a few yards away on top of those of the dead soldiers the Japanese had killed before charging into the tent.

The nurses tried to protect themselves by holding onto each other in a tight pack, crying and screaming with fear, transfixed, as the two doctors and the few soldiers that were there to protect them were dragged out of the tent. The doctors shouted. 'We are medical doctors,' pointing to the stethoscopes around their necks. The Japanese responded by forcing the doctors to kneel, they were held down while one of the Japanese drew a knife across their throats. Gilda was nearest to the opening of the torn tent and deliberately blocked the horrific scene from the other nurse's view, she saw the doctor's heads rolling to one side, partially decapitated. Only two soldiers, part of the group who were posted to guard the nurses, were left. The Japanese tied them to wooden posts and used them for bayonet charges. The shrill screams of the men as their bodies were repeatedly pierced, echoed off the surrounding trees but their screams only served to excite the Japanese who carried out further atrocities on their bodies before, mercifully, they died.

The Allies had a comprehensive stock of food and medical supplies in the field stations, while the Japanese had practically none. They had been cut off from their own supply units owing to the Allied soldiers advancing forward and pushing the retreating, starving enemy back towards Rangoon, the Japanese soldiers lost no time in ransacking the Allies' supplies.

Gilda and the nurses, in their scanty party dresses, were frozen with fear as the Japanese soldiers who were in the tent viewed them with mouth-watering lust and dragged the screaming nurses onto the beds. Gilda, with her long blonde hair, was the great attraction and was first to be stripped naked and raped. The nurses continued screaming as their clothes were ripped off and were raped repeatedly.

For twenty-four hours the nurses suffered rape and multiple forms of sexual abuse. Gilda was tortured with every form of bestial sexual deviation and raped continuously. Her long, blonde hair was cut off and taken as souvenirs by soldiers who had never seen such bright blonde hair before. Gilda's head was left with just a few tufts of hair.

After the savage mass orgy, and before leaving the tent, the Japanese soldiers killed the nurses by bayoneting them to death. Gilda was presumed to be dead as her body was covered with blood and body waste, her eyes were widely open staring into space, and her faint breathing undetected beneath the filth on her body.

The silence outside the tent was surreal after the barbarous sexual assault, and it left Gilda drifting in and out of consciousness. In her subconscious state she held her hands high under her Spreading Chestnut Tree, waiting, not knowing for what; was she dead, was this a terrible nightmare, where was she?

Morning came, and Gilda stirred herself into consciousness, she thought she heard familiar voices. They were not Japanese, who were they, and why were they in my dream. 'Jesus Christ,' said a voice, 'over here lads.' And suddenly soldiers once again entered the tent.

The soldier who had called out, was Sergeant Liam Kennedy of the Fourteenth Army. He oversaw fifty Chindits, all that was left of his company. Chindits were special forces operating behind enemy lines. His officers and men having been killed or had succumbed to the hazards of the jungle, fighting the Japanese, dying of fever, snake bites. exhaustion, and a catalogue of other deadly infections.

Sergeant Kennedy and his remaining men were making their way to a dropping zone called Broadway, and then to India.

'They're all dead,' said Kennedy. 'All these poor souls are all bloody dead,' he shouted, and looked about him wanting to kill someone.

The soldiers began to take the bodies of the nurses out of the tent, when a soldier heard a groan coming from one of the beds. 'Please don't hurt me.' It was the murmured plea, when he looked at the nurse more closely, whom he first thought to be dead, he saw that she was holding her side which had been pierced by a bayonet. The caked blood from the wound had helped to disguise the fact that she was still alive. The soldier felt embarrassed by her nudity and quickly covered her up with a towel and then a blanket which he found beneath one of the beds.

'Quiet,' shouted Kennedy, as he moved slowly towards Gilda. He bent down and saw her eyes move and he heard the faint, whispered murmuring words of a song he remembered from his Boy Scout days sitting round the campfire, "Underneath the Spreading Chestnut Tree".

'This one's alive, hurry up and get a bowl of hot water, towels, anything, but hurry up.' Checks were made to see if any of the other nurses were still alive, but there was only

Gilda and one other. The dead nurses were laid alongside the dead soldiers and the two dead doctors.

Kennedy and his men were shocked by the state of Gilda. Kennedy started to call for orderlies and first aid kits, then realised that he was in a medical jungle unit and there might be some first aid packs that the Japanese had missed. The Chindits had no doctors or orderlies and carried limited packs containing first aid kits. When wounded, they were left behind with just enough ammunition to kill themselves and avoid being taken prisoner by the Japanese and tortured, or, if possible, collected by their colleagues should the company return.

The two surviving nurses were later identified by one of Kennedy's men. He called out softly, 'Sarge.' Kennedy looked round at the soldier who dared to break the silence in this killing field. 'We found identity discs on the nurses; their names were—'

'Shush,' Kennedy said, holding up his left arm, his right hand resting on Gilda's head. The soldier then produced a photograph of Gilda which was amongst the ransacked nurse's equipment found in the nurse's tent.

'Her name was, sorry Sarge, I mean her name is Gilda Marchant, and she was a cracker.' Kennedy looked at the picture and turned his head back to the woman lying in front of him. He, a grown man, trained to kill, combat experienced, knelt beside her, stroked her practically bald head and cried. 'Sarge,' said the soldier, even more quietly. He too was traumatised by the scene of torture and torment laid out before him. 'The other nurse's name is Beattie Beardsley.'

Beattie was washed and wiped, as best as possible, her wounds were cleansed and covered up. And then she was wrapped up with the cleanest towels that could be found. Her speech was painfully soft, but as she became aware that the soldiers around her were English, her confidence returned, and her voice became firmer. Kennedy called out for clothes to be found amongst the scattered debris left behind in the tents by the Japs. Beattie was carried away from the killing tent on a stretcher to a tent that had been made more habitable out of sight from the dreadful carnage that had taken place.

Gilda had internal wounds which needed hospital attention, but meantime, Sergeant Kennedy examined her and removed bamboo canes inserted between her blood coated legs. He shouted, 'Fetch that bloody water, and find some more women's clothing.' They transferred Gilda to a clean bed, made ready by the other men who were all equally appalled at what they had just witnessed. Kennedy and his men were overwhelmed by emotion at the agony that Gilda had obviously had to endure. One soldier fainted and two ran out and vomited. Covered in blood, Japanese body fluids over her body, haircut and torn from her head, it was impossible to comprehend such vile behaviour by a human being; this was subhuman.

A screen was hastily made and placed around Gilda. As her mind wondered, she feared she was about to be raped again. She prepared herself to succumb to another ordeal; she did not know if she was alive or dead. She felt something on her body, but it was not the heavy, sweaty, smelly body of her many rapists, it was cool and smooth, moving up her neck. It was not the foul breath of a man poised to hurt her. It was a gentle hand which stroked her head. She felt warm water wiping her body, she smelt disinfectant cleansing her. Voices seemed kindly and familiar.

Kennedy and another soldier were still in the process of tending to Gilda when the tramping of feet and many voices with accents from India, Australia, and America were heard, and again soldiers entered the tent, but this time they were officers. Kennedy stood up and saluted, puzzled at their arrival, and apologised for not wearing his hat. He looked out of the tent and saw many soldiers kitted up and accompanied by motor transport.

'At ease sergeant,' said one of the officers. 'I'm Lieutenant Ryan, Doctor Michael Ryan.' He explained how he had met with this mix of soldiers, of different nationalities, who were part of the advance on Rangoon, a major assault planned to surround the Japanese and allow allied ships and landing craft to enter and relieve Rangoon and make access to the harbour easy and safe for troops to land. Michael Ryan and the officers with him could not help but notice the poor condition of Kennedy and his Chindits.

Chindits had been dropped behind Japanese lines and had fought the Japanese for months in the wet monsoon season, May to November. They had no change of clothes and, after months in the wet and humid jungle, those that they wore were in tatters. They had been surviving on emergency food supplies for those in the front line, a three-day provision which was infrequently replenished for soldiers in the jungle, miles away from the supply drop zones.

Dysentery, malaria, jungle foot rot, leeches scarring their limbs, and blow flies covering their food and clothes, were just some of the debilitating illnesses and conditions to which they were exposed. Those with sudden and extreme attacks of dysentery would split the seats of their trousers to ease their discomfort. Their plight was obvious to the new arrivals at the field hospital.

Doctor Ryan took Kennedy to one side and explained that he was travelling up country to a drop zone called Broadway, where a Dakota was due to land in three days' time. Kennedy informed Ryan, that he too, was attempting to reach Broadway in time to catch his "bus" to India.

Ryan had six patients with him, but he offered to accommodate the two nurses and at a push some of Kennedy's men including six of the worst sufferers in his company. He had the use of an American 6x6 Dodge truck to cover the hundred miles to the drop zone. He pointed out that the Dakota was off loading fresh troops and, if Kennedy could push his men, they might also make it through the jungle to Broadway.

Gilda was a problem for Michael Ryan. She could not speak or make any sign of recognition as he tended her wounds and sedated her for the rough journey. They had to travel through the jungle, slowed down by the mud rutted wheel tracks, on roads that vanished in the quagmire of rain, mud up to the axels, always aware that they could be ambushed by the Japanese at any moment.

Beattie, however, was pulling herself together, and even on that roller coaster journey, she was able to talk to Dr Michael Ryan. "Michael", as he had told her to call him. Her description of the treatment meted out to Gilda that Christmas day was a horror story. Ryan looked back in wonder at Gilda, lying on a stretcher oblivious to everything that was going on in the truck around her, the rocking bumps, the sliding wheels and the cursing of the men. Just as well, as they all slept and cooked in the truck, toilet stops were made with pots and buckets as no one dared to stop the truck or leave it for any purpose at all in case it got stuck in the mud.

Meanwhile Kennedy, relieved of his obligations to the sick and wounded, was making good headway and hoped to make the journey to Broadway on time to catch his "bus", his main worry being whether the Japs would spring an ambush.

Ryan's Dodge truck arrived at the Broadway Drop Zone with a day to spare and they were met by several heavily armed American airmen who were guarding and supervising the dropping zone. They informed Ryan that the expected Dakota DC3–C47 would be about two days late, as it was necessary first to clear the area of logs deliberately laid across the drop zone by the Burmese loggers in the jungle.

Although disappointed at the delay, it did give Ryan and the passengers in the truck nearly three days in which to wash, stretch their legs and attend to their wounds and various ailments.

Late one night, two days after their arrival, they were all alerted and quickly armed as they heard noises coming out of the jungle; they prepared themselves to face a Japanese patrol, only to be greeted by a haggard but smiling Sergeant Liam Kennedy, who thought that he had missed his bus to India, but in fact had brought his depleted company safely to the Broadway Drop Zone.

The DC3–C47 Dakota was the workhorse of Burma and, during the Second World War, was the most versatile aircraft, it's uses included the landing on short jungle air strips, delivering supplies such as arms and small trucks to the troops, and acting as an air ambulance. In Europe, as in Burma, it was used by airborne troops and for the evacuation of the wounded and the sick. On this occasion it was bringing in supplies and fresh troops to join the advancing armies into Rangoon and evacuate the sick and wounded to India.

Part Two

Gilda, Lieutenant Doctor Michael Ryan, as he had become and Beattie were in India for two months and were all eventually repatriated to England. When the ship carrying them arrived in Liverpool, they were shepherded to waiting ambulances by medical teams along with other sick and wounded patients, all victims of the Far Eastern Campaign, and then transferred to hospitals around the country.

Michael Ryan, Gilda and Beattie were greeted by medical staff from Mallard House Hospital MOD, a quiet convalescent home for the armed forces, which overlooked the cliffs and the sea at Membury in the county of Hampshire. It served as a place of recuperation for those still in a state of mental shock, now recognised as post traumatic distress cases; unfortunately, at that time, the locals called it a lunatic asylum. There were psychiatrists at Mallard who were trained to treat severe conditions of mental disorder, and it was hoped that such treatment would restore Gilda and help her to face the world again.

Michael and Beattie had become overly attached to one another during the time spent in India. On the ship sailing home, they were frequently seen together, arm-in-arm, walking along the deck and often going into Michael's cabin. Gilda was usually to be found sitting in her cabin alone, just staring into space. Sometimes she could be heard humming the tune, "Underneath the Spreading Chestnut Tree". Beattie explained to Michael that it was the last time and the last words that Gilda had spoken.

On arrival at Mallard House Gilda was given a room with panoramic views over the cliffs and the sea. It was suggested that the serene atmosphere and views might help her to recover.

The day after their arrival at Mallard House Michael and Beattie received an urgent call to go to the office of the senior doctor, Major Letchworth. He informed them that he was a gynaecologist as well as general physician, and that after examining Gilda's wounds and assessing her mental state he found that she was pregnant. Beattie fainted whilst Michael stood glued to the ground shocked and white-faced. When everybody had recovered from the shock of learning of Gilda's pregnancy, the question in all their minds was, what to do next?

Major Letchworth put two courses of action to them that could be taken, and which one of those might be the better of the two. He explained that if the pregnancy were aborted it could have an adverse effect on Gilda, and that in fact the operation might kill her. The other option would be to let the pregnancy take its course, in which case the birth would possibly be in August or September 1945. It was decided not to risk her life.

Gilda could often be seen walking along the public footpath on the cliff top just a few minutes away from Mallard House or sitting on a wooden bench that directly faced the sea. The sound of the sea and the pleasant summer breeze had a tranquil, calming effect on her. Beattie would sometimes accompany Gilda, they just sat together in silence, each in their own secret world. Beattie remembered the early days of the war when they both danced and sang their way through the Blitz in the dance halls of London. And enlisting into the Queen Alexandra Military Nursing School then being posted to the Far East, India and then Burma.

Beattie and Michael announced that they were to be married, which was providential, as there was a cottage in the grounds of Mallard House which had been empty for some time and would serve admirably as married quarters for the couple. Michael would eventually become senior doctor of Mallard Home and Beattie, as a Queen Alexander trained nurse, became his senior nurse and Hospital Matron.

Beattie and Michael were married in June and invited the hospital staff and patients as guests to the wedding reception, which was to be held in a marquee in the grounds of Mallard House. It was a perfect summer's day. Gilda was being helped to dress by the nursing sisters who were given clothes for the purpose from Beattie's own wardrobe. Gilda and Beattie had been friends before, as well as during the war, and they often exchanged, as well as shared their clothes, as they were the same height and size.

Towards the end of July Gilda was obviously approaching the end of her pregnancy. The whole hospital was on edge, everybody worried whether Gilda would live through the trauma of giving birth.

When the time came, Beattie held her hand and felt Gilda squeeze it, whilst the matron, a trained midwife, delivered the child. The room was full of nurses waiting in anticipation of how Gilda would react to the birth. Michael looked at Beattie and winked as the baby was delivered, a girl. The baby was a most beautiful child, shiny black hair, clear light olive skin, her little face the picture of an eastern princess, with slanting eyes and tulip lips.

When the new-born baby had been cleaned and wrapped up in a shawl, Michael, Major Letchworth and several the nurses watched as Beattie took the child over to Gilda and placed her near to the new mother's face.

Gilda's face changed into one of horror, contorted as she screamed with fright. The face that she saw was that of the Japanese soldiers who had raped and tortured her. Beattie pulled the baby sharply away from Gilda and Michael took the child from her. Beattie looked at Michael, her face streaming with tears. Beattie knew that she would never have children, because the torture she had endured at the hands of the Japanese had put paid to that. That Gilda had been able to conceive, after the abuse she had suffered, was a miracle. Beattie went over to Gilda, placed her arms around her friend, cuddling her like a child, and together they wept. The nurses and doctors left the room, most of them in tears. Michael kissed Beattie's head and he too left. The midwife took the child away and prepared to nurse the baby. Late that night Michael held Beattie close to him as they lay in bed. 'Beattie,' he said, 'the baby must have a name, and be baptised.'

Gilda kept to her room for a week after giving birth, whilst the nurses took it in turns to bottle feed the child and one of them slept in an adjoining room in case the child should wake up and cry.

Ten days after Gilda had given birth, the night nurse was woken up at five in the morning by what sounded like muffled singing. She went to where the baby slept, which had become known as the nursery room, but the cot was empty. She shouted out loud, 'The baby's gone.' Alarm bells were rung, and the staff ran to Gilda's room, but Gilda too was gone. One of the nurses phoned Michael and Beattie in their cottage and they quickly emerged in their night clothes. As they came out of the cottage, they were shocked to see Gilda in the centre of the large rose garden which separated it from Mallard House. The circular rose garden was dissected by a path cutting through its centre.

In that short time many of the staff and patients had assembled round the perimeter of the garden and were standing silently, all eyes on Gilda, the baby in her arms. Gilda was kissing and hugging the warmly wrapped child while she whispered a nursery rhyme, 'Suki put the Kettle on, Suki put the kettle on.' But of course, the nursery rhyme was, "Polly put the kettle on", not "Suki put the Kettle on". Did Gilda know that the meaning of the name Suki in Japanese is "One who is loved"? She might have learnt it during her time in the Far East treating patients of all nationalities. She repeated the same few words of the song over and over.

Then, very slowly, Gilda turned and walked very slowly towards Beattie. When she was close, she took Beattie's hand and led her along the cliff footpath to the bench where they had both sat, looking out to sea during her pregnancy. As Beattie sat down on the bench, Gilda kissed her baby and in the full sight of the doctors and patients who had followed the two women along the footpath, she handed her to Beattie. The watchers kept a short distance, so as not to disturb the magical moment. Then Gilda bent over and kissed Beattie's head and shouted, 'Name my baby Suki.' And in one swift movement, she turned and leapt over the cliff, falling two hundred feet into the sea, her white nightdress billowing out like the wings of a white dove as she flew through the air, her hands outstretched like her Spreading Chestnut Tree.

The local newspapers reported that a patient of Mallard House had committed suicide. It did not arouse much interest until the story of Gilda's treatment at the hands of the Japanese in the Burmese Jungle was published, which came about after Michael Ryan had spoken to the editors of the local papers. They then published a full account of the atrocities against the nurses by the Japanese in the field hospitals in Burma. The National press soon picked up on that story and it became of great national interest and concern. Gilda's death was formally recorded by Military officials, not as death by suicide, but in military terms "DOW" – Died of Wounds received in action – as indeed it was and should have been. Arrangements were made for Gilda to be given a full military funeral in the small church cemetery in Membury. But before that took place a baptism was held in the small chapel in Mallard House. Gilda's baby was named Suki Marchant.

Shortly afterwards, the phone rang in the cottage; Beattie picked it up and the voice at the other end said, 'You might not remember me, but my name is Liam Kennedy, and I was in the field hospital.' Before he could say any more, Beattie called Michael and they both spoke at the same time to Kennedy, sharing the mouthpiece of the telephone.

Kennedy told them that he had lost touch with most people after they had disembarked in Liverpool. In the confusion that followed, with so many soldiers being transferred to different parts of the country, himself amongst them, he had lost touch with his friends and comrades. He only managed to contact them after he had read about Gilda's death in the National press. He, and some of his Chindit comrades, wanted to be at Gilda's funeral. The people of Membury changed their attitude to the so called "lunatic asylum" and showed their feelings and remorse by laying wreaths outside Mallard House; they too said that they wanted to attend the funeral.

Nurses from the same unit that Beattie and Gilda belonged to in Burma arrived early in the morning on the day of the funeral, followed by several soldiers who had served in the Far East. There was a bugler who said that it was an honour to play the Last Post at Gilda's funeral, which complemented the full military honours conferred on her with a gun salute fired by a Guard of Honour.

The interest in Gilda's death raised by the publicity in the National press, resulted in the funeral being attended by hundreds of people; a military Padre conducted the ceremony extolling the bravery of nurses in frontline medical units. There were very few dry eyes after his eulogy to Gilda.

Beattie and Michael became guardians to Suki who lived with them in the cottage. What was to be of great benefit was the fact that a fund had been set up for Suki by the National newspapers until she was fully educated.

To help her raise Suki, Beattie employed a Nanny/housekeeper, named Ruth. Nanny Ruth, as she was known, cleaned and cooked and, when needed, she would sleep in the cottage overnight, particularly when Beattie and Michael were away at conferences.

During Suki's half term holiday from school in 1957, when she was aged twelve, Michael and Beattie had to go up to London to attend a conference related to the treatment of tropical diseases at the British Medical Council. As they had both served in the jungles in the Far East, where thousands of servicemen died through the lack of adequate treatment, they were able to give first-hand evidence of what was needed by way of up-to-date treatment and appropriate antibiotics.

Suki had grown into a beautiful young lady. Michael and Beattie were immensely proud of her, particularly as she had passed all her exams at school with distinction. Suki knew that they were not her birth parents and called them both by their first names and the household was an incredibly happy one. Suki frequently went to her mother's grave in the church yard and read the inscription on the headstone; Gilda Marchant, Nurse, Died of her wounds, August 1945.

It was while Michael and Beattie were away at a British Medical Council meeting that Suki took herself off to visit her mother's grave early one morning when the dew was still lying on the grass. Nanny Ruth had told her that when she returned, they would sit down and have lunch together.

Suki came back and had the promised lunch and then she pottered about the cottage for a while. She went into the study where Michael kept his medical records, photo albums and biographies all packed onto his bookshelves and not in any order. Among the clutter of box files there was one with the name of Gilda written in ink on the binding. It aroused her curiosity and she pulled it down from the shelf.

Nanny Ruth was resting in the armchair listening to the radio when she heard screams coming from the study; she rushed in to see Suki surrounded by the contents of the box file, crying and banging her head on the carpet floor.

Reports and records, photos and tufts of blonde hair were scattered over the floor. There were photos of Gilda and Beattie, taken by Liam Kennedy with a bellows Coronet camera. It was easy to carry, and it was the one which Liam always carried with him to record life in the jungle. The pictures showed the condition in which Kennedy had found Gilda and Beattie when he came upon them after Christmas in 1944. Suki read some of the reports, including the one which described Gilda's reaction on seeing her child for the first time and rejecting her. Nanny Ruth hugged Suki to her breast rocking her like a baby, and that is how they stayed, on the carpet surrounded with the ghostly past of her mother, until Beattie and Michael came home that night and heard sobs coming from the study. No one slept that night, nor did Suki speak; she kept to her room, her bedroom door wide open and stared into oblivion. Beattie held and fed her like a baby.

Two days after Suki discovered the history of her mother's suffering at the hands of the Japanese and of that moment of rejection, Suki told Beattie that she wanted to see where Gilda, her mother, had leapt off the cliff. Much as Beattie and Michael did not want to go there, they decided reluctantly to do as Suki had asked. Hand in hand they walked slowly along the cliff top public foot path. They sat on the same bench that Beattie and Gilda sat on and watched the tide ebbing and flowing against the base of the cliffs.

After a while Suki released their hands from hers, stood up and cried. 'I'm going to Gilda, my mummy.' She ran to the edge of the cliff and leapt off into the air.

In the mist and the spray beneath them, did Beattie and Michael see hands reach out above the Chestnut Tree, to catch Suki? They would always miss Gilda and Suki and hope that they were now together.

None of the characters are real. The names of some of the places have been changed. There is no recovery hospital by the name of Mallard House. But atrocities of the type described in this story did take place.

http://members.iinet.au-gduncan/massacres_pacific.htm

http://www.qaranc.co.uk/bmh_Bowen_Road_Hong_Kong.php

Fourteenth Army in Burma.

Field Hospitals in the Far East

Doolittle's raid on Tokyo

Stephen's Onion

Chapter One

Stephen was a victim of a pandemic flu plague and had been confined to his bed for three weeks. His parents, Renata and Mathew Oglethorpe, were not sure whether their 23-year-old son should have been hospitalised, as the plague was spreading out of control throughout the country, and throughout the world. Patients were dying of the plague in hospitals without the comfort of having visitors, even the closest families were not allowed to visit their dying loved ones. Stephen was very weak, tired and breathless. With his head resting on the pillow, he accepted his fate, that he would probably die very soon. His mother and father became his own nurses, administering medication, which consisted of applying oxygen masks whenever Stephen had difficulty in breathing, placing cold towels on his head when he felt hot, and bathing him with anti-bacterial soap and wipes. They had visited their local medical surgery for advice but felt that they had been rebuffed. 'His illness is not serious enough for him to be hospitalised,' said their doctor, Bartolomeu Hicks. An elderly doctor, who never attempted to keep up with the advances in medical treatment, or attend upgrading lectures at the British Medical Association. He did not have a good doctor patient relationship or a bedside manner. His surgery was akin to a conveyor belt in a factory, his patients were in and out of his surgery so fast that it was a wonder whether he ever gave the correct prescriptions to the right patient. The impression he gave was that of a reluctant tired medical practitioner at the end of his working life, just looking forward to his retirement and medical pension, and the quicker that retirement came the better. Stephen's mother looked at the doctor with contempt and said, 'You are a pathetic moronic excuse for a doctor and should be struck off.' Stephen's parents took it upon themselves to care for their son by taking extreme precautions, when they entered his bedroom, they cloaked themselves in protective clothes, masks, gloves, antiseptic wipes and spray. They nursed him and prayed for a healing miracle vaccine.

Chapter Two

The night sky was ablaze with stars, the bright shining moon in all its glory appeared to float and dance across the stars as if the stars were steppingstones.

Stephen felt that he had to see this phenomenon. The curtains in his bedroom had been drawn back by his mother, as she too had seen early on in the evening the formation of stars as had never been seen before, and she wanted to share this heavenly picture with her son. Stephen, weak though he was, dragged his coughing, sweaty body across the room from his bed to the window, with his elbows resting on the window ledge and his hands clasped together beneath his chin, supporting his head. He felt an urge to engage in this heavenly display and dance among the stars. Looking up at this galactic star-studded display in the sky, he noticed a red coloured cloud breaking away from the stars and watched as it began to float down towards the earth. The cloud seemed to hesitate, hovering and floating in the sky not sure which way to go. At the same time, its shape was changing from a ragged mountainous looking cloud to a form that looked like a large red onion. Stephen scratched his head and questioned the fact that this cloud had a mind of its own and was thinking about which direction it might take. It began to move again much moe slowly than before. As it progressed towards the earth it grew larger and larger. Stephen began to feel a throbbing all over his body, he felt as if that the cloud was trying to communicate with him. When he stared at the cloud it seemed to stare back at him. The red cloud descended and settled like a blanket over the Oglethorpe house.

Chapter Three

The next morning at 8 am there was a disturbance in the kitchen with the sound of pots, pans and china being pushed around. The noise wakened Renata and Mathew, who were still in bed. Mathew, thinking that there was a burglar in the house, told Renata to call the police. He got out of bed and crept silently down the stairs, at the bottom of which there was a broom cupboard. Mathew quietly opened the cupboard, removed a broom, expecting to use it as a weapon. Broom in his hand he approached the kitchen and as he apprehensively swung the door open the sight before him made him stand rock solid still in amazement and shock.

Busy making tea and toast for the family was Stephen, singing, and smiling. He stopped what he was doing and ran to his father throwing his arms around him. They both said nothing, their hugging arms, tears and smiles did all the talking.

Renata in her nightdress, entered the kitchen and stood absolutely still as she focused her eyes on her family, jumping with joy and laughing.

How, why, and if did this miracle happen? Stephen led his parents up the stairs to his bedroom. The smell that hit them as they entered, the room was of rotten onions. 'Look over there,' said Renata. She was pointing to the bedside table on top of which were three large onions, as black as pitch.

'Don't touch them,' said his father. 'I believe that those onions have absorbed the virus, and that they will have to be burnt.' The previous moments of joy were over as they faced the problem of disposing of the black infested onions. Not wishing to touch the onions without protective clothing. Mathew told Stephen to wait in the lounge whilst he and Renata decided how to carry these diseased ridden onions into the garden. With their usual protective clothes, which they had been wearing when entering Stephen's bedroom, and an assortment of plastic bags, they tentatively lifted the onions and placed them in the plastic bags. Mathew took the deadly packages to the end of the garden where there was a fire pit. The pit, which was used to burn waste rubbish, was, this time, going to burn the cause of their son's illness, the deadly flu.

'Here's a bottle of paraffin.' Renata held out the bottle of oil at arm's length, not daring to approach near to the deadly package. Mathew slowly lowered the plastic bag into the fire pit. Taking the bottle from Renata he poured the contents of it into the pit covering the plastic bags. Renata gave him a tightly rolled newspaper which he used as a taper, not wishing to be near to the contents of the fire pit.

'Here it goes,' said Mathew. With that, he threw the taper into the pit and they both watched as the flames engulfed the bags and their contents. Stephen, looking through the lounge window, observed this act of defiance by his loving parents against this deadly virus and thought they were being very brave.